PARANORMAL STORIES MORGUE

EVE S EVANS

ALSO BY EVE S EVANS

Fiction:

The Haunting of Hartley House
Hartley House Homecoming
The Haunting of Crow House
The Haunting of Redburn Manor
Origins
Beneath The Water
Mistletoe Magic
The Haunting of Lila Lamm
Willed

Anthologies:

True Ghost Stories of First Responders
50 Terrifying Ghost Stories
Holiday Hauntings
Shadow People
Chilling Ghost Stories
Haunted Hotels
Haunted Hospitals
Haunted Objects
Paranormal Pets
Haunted on Vacation
Haunted Murder Houses
Real Ghost Stories: Southern Hauntings
Supernatural 911 Calls
Demonic Hauntings
When I Died

"After death, you rest and then decide where you wish to go next."

— UNKNOWN

FOLLOW EVE ── ON ── BOOKBUB OR GOODREADS

AND GET NOTIFIED OF ALL NEW READS COMING IN 2023-2023.

THE FOLLOWING STORIES ARE BASED ON TRUE EVENTS.

ALL RIGHTS RESERVED.

No part of this publication may be transmitted or reproduced in any form or by any means. This includes photocopying, electronic, mechanical, or by storage system (informational or otherwise), unless given written permission by the author.

Copyright © February 2023 Eve S. Evans

CHAPTER

1

PROXIMITY

As a funeral home director, I'm used to dealing with both the living and the dead. Families rely on me to make sure their loved ones are handled with the care and respect that they deserve. Despite my proximity with the dead, I'd never had any so-called paranormal experiences, and wasn't much of a believer in life after death. That was, until something happened that completely changed that.

I was on my way to the morgue to pick up a body, which itself wasn't an unusual occurrence. But my assistant who normally handled the pick-ups was unavailable, so this time I had to go myself.

The morgue was inside an older part of the local hospital, and I always hated having to walk down the long, dark corridors to get there. There was very rarely anyone down there except for the mortician on duty, so the sound of my footsteps echoing around the gloom was a little unsettling, even for a middle-aged man such as myself.

There was nobody at the front desk, but I managed to flag down the mortician as she was coming out of the autopsy rooms, pulling off a pair of latex gloves and tossing them into the bin.

I'd seen her here before and she seemed to recognize me too, so she led me into a cramped office where I showed her my documentation for the body I was picking up.

"Of course, wait right here, and I'll go get the body ready," she told me, before marching off and leaving me alone in the stuffy office.

A few moments later, the grating of wheels against linoleum drifted down the corridor, and I stepped out to greet her. Only there was nobody there; the corridor was empty. I could have sworn I'd heard the grind of trolley wheels, but the moment I stepped out of the office, everything went silent.

Weird.

I decided to wait out in the corridor instead, and eventually the mortician appeared at the doorway at the end. When she saw me, she gestured for me to follow her, and led me past the autopsy rooms and into the mortuary chamber.

"Sorry, there seems to be a bit of a mix up with the paperwork," she told me after flicking through some sheafs of documents. "Give me a moment and I'll go find the right ones."

She disappeared once again, leaving me alone.

I'd been in the mortuary many times before, but the cold metal and eerie stillness of the cadaver storage still had me shifting uncomfortably as I waited for the mortician to return.

I had my back to the cadaver cold storage cabinet and was fiddling with the watch on my wrist when I heard the distinct sound of a lock disengaging, and the cold hiss of air escaping the freezer.

I turned with a start to see one of the metal doors swing open, a few metres away from me.

My heart dropped into my stomach, and a sense of ice-cold dread filled me as I half-expected the drawer to slide out. But that didn't happen. After a few beats of staring at the open door, I went to investigate.

There was no possibility of these drawers opening by themselves, since the handle had to be turned completely to the right to disengage the seal, otherwise the temperature wouldn't be consistent.

And yet I was the only one here. The door had opened by itself, no doubt.

I peered inside, but luckily there wasn't a body in there; just a long stretch of empty darkness.

Swallowing back my unease, I closed the door and made sure it was properly locked this time. Perhaps it had simply been loose, and gravity had done the rest.

Footsteps tapped against the floor behind me, and I quickly straightened, about to explain to the mortician what I was doing, but found myself stopping short as I turned round.

The mortician hadn't returned yet. There was nobody else here.

But those footsteps… had I imagined them?

I wanted to believe I was just being silly or paranoid, but it left me feeling more than unsettled, and I hoped the mortician would be back soon.

Moving away from the cadaver storage drawers, I loitered around one of the metal autopsy tables, trying to ignore the feeling that I wasn't alone in here. Despite trying to retain my sense of professionalism, I found myself chewing anxiously on the inside of my gum, listening for the faintest sound of footsteps coming down the corridor.

Tapping my fingers against my elbow, I saw something move out of the corner of my eye, and turned just as something clattered off the table, bouncing off my shoe and landing a few inches away.

A medical scalpel.

My eyes traced the path from the metal tray sitting innocuously on the side, to the scalpel now lying on the floor, trying to work out how it had managed to fall off on its own.

I hadn't been anywhere near the table or the tray, so it wasn't like I'd accidentally knocked it. The scalpel had fallen on its own, in some inexplicable fashion.

Scratching my head, I bent down to pick it up, setting it back on the side.

When I glanced up again, someone was standing at the doorway.

"Jesus," I blurted, clutching my chest as the mortician stepped inside. "You scared me."

She offered me a crooked smile. "Sorry," she said. "It's that kind of place, huh?"

I merely nodded as she came over with a folder of documents, eager to get out of here as soon as possible.

Once we'd checked everything was as it should be, the mortician got the body out of cold storage and transferred them onto a gurney for easy transportation. The grinding of the wheels reminded me of the incident earlier, but I tried not to think about it as I thanked her for her help.

The back entrance of the morgue led directly into the staff parking lot, which made loading bodies into the hearse a quick and easy task. One of the hospital staff helped me wheel the trolley out into the lot, and I started to load it into the back of the car for transport.

"I can take it from here, thank you," I told him, watching him head inside before turning back to the hearse.

Just as I finished loading the body into the vehicle, a cold breath ran down my neck, and my whole body froze as a male voice whispered 'thank you' beside my ear.

Startled, I turned around, wondering if the hospital worker had returned, but there was nobody else around me.

I wanted to tell myself I'd simply imagined it, but the voice had been too clear, too *real* for me to have simply conjured it.

Making sure everything was fastened securely, I closed the lid and hurried into the driver's seat. The whole way back to the funeral home, I played the events over in my mind, but I was unable to truly understand any of it, or what it meant.

As a funeral director, I'm used to rationalizing death and its inevitability, but I can't deny there's always a faint sense of curiosity about what it's really like to pass from this world. Is there anything waiting on the other side? It is one of the many mysteries that we will never truly know until it's our own time. But being in this line of work does give you a deeper glimpse into that world than usual, and what I experienced that day at the morgue gave me the smallest nudge towards the answer of what the true reality of death might be.

CHAPTER

2

Patients From The Past

For a few of the years I was growing up my family lived in a small town in the eastern part of the United States. Most of the homes were older and came with a past, ours was no exception. In fact the house we lived in happened to be the location of the doctor's office and the temporary morgue over a hundred years ago. Needless to say, when you're 10 years old your parents don't tend to mention this to you in hopes your imagination run wild.

The first two nights there had been the worst. Sleep had come in fits and starts that left me more tired than I had been when I'd turned my lights off. I'd even told my parents that I was going to sleep during the day where at least the sun could protect me, and I could keep watch during the nighttime. Both of them got a chuckle from this which resulted in me storming back to my room and the slamming of the door.

It took us living there just over a week before I felt comfortable in there by myself. The "New House" jitters hadn't fully dissipated but I was starting to know the sounds the house made during the night when everyone else was asleep. At least now the creaking and flexing of the old wood didn't have me jumping up thinking someone was about to come into my room. That feeling of home didn't last long though.

Two weeks to the day we moved in I had been up late watching some television when I heard a noise like someone was walking up the stairs to where my brother and my rooms were. My parents had gone to sleep a while ago, but it wasn't out of character for them to check on the two of us at night.

My room was the first one they'd pass in the hall so I wrapped my blanket around me and turned on my side hoping to look asleep when they went by. I opened my eyes enough to peek towards the door so I could see if they'd bought my ruse when I saw something that had the breath freeze in my throat. I wanted to look away, but I couldn't bring myself to do so.

The figure of a man in a long coat passed right in front of my door. I knew immediately I wasn't looking at someone who was alive. First of all, he emitted a glow that didn't seem to spread anywhere except around his body. His face, although male would fade in and out of focus as if he was having trouble keeping his form. But the thing that told me this wasn't a living person was despite the sound of footsteps, the bottom half of his legs was missing below the knees. Despite this though he moved as if he could walk normally.

I willed myself not to move in hopes he wouldn't notice me. Despite my efforts though the adrenaline in my veins sent tremors through my entire body. The image only lasted a matter of a second or two but it felt like it stretched on for much longer.

I sat there in bed and listened as the sound of his footsteps moved farther down the hall towards my brother's room. Through the wall that our rooms shared I heard *him* walking around as if circling my brother's bed. That was the moment I found my voice.

I screamed for my mom and dad as loud as I could. This time when footsteps could be heard coming up the stairs, they were loud and at high speed, not the quiet measured tones that came from the spirit. My dad burst into my room follow close behind by my mom. The lights came on and I saw him look in every corner assessing for threats.

I was bawling when they came over to me. I was trying to tell them I saw a man in the hall and heard him go into my brother's room but I couldn't get anything out but a jumbled mess of broken words and sobbing noises.

That is when I heard my brother come into my

room and ask what was going on. The relief I felt when I saw him was indescribable and it finally allowed me to calm down enough to tell my parents what I'd seen and heard. The most frustrating part of that was they asserted that I must have been dreaming and had woken up confused.

"Look, your brother is right over there and he's fine, okay?" they kept repeating in hopes that I'd agree with them.

I wanted to believe that was really what happened, but I wasn't a child prone to hysterics. I'd never claimed to have an imaginary friend and at 10 years old I thought I was old enough to tell the difference between what is real and what was a dream. In the end they did their best to settle my nerves and left the light on out in the hall so I could see there was no one there.

This wasn't the only occurrence of unexplainable things that happened while we were living there. To my relief every instance seemed to center around my brother's room rather than my own. If it had been mine, I would have insisted on sleeping somewhere else in the house.

About a year after I'd seen the ghost in the hallway I was having a hard time getting to sleep when I heard the sound of a man and a woman talking to each other coming through the vent in the wall. In the past I could hear my brother's television through this, and I figured that he might still be awake.

Standing on top of the bed I tried to listen to what was being said. Now that I could hear better, I realized it was two people having an argument, but there words were odd almost like they were speaking some other language, one that I'd never heard before.

Curious I crept over to my brother's door and peeked in hoping maybe we could talk for a bit to relax my mind a bit. What I saw though didn't make sense. I could see the slow rise and fall of his chest. He was obviously fast asleep. I was sure I'd heard people talking in here but there was no one here.

To this day I don't really have a lot of great

memories from that place. I can say when we moved out after a couple of years, I've never been so happy to pack up and leave. My parents and brother may not believe me that those things happened but I'm convinced that house held onto something that was never intended to stay there.

CHAPTER

3

Help Me

Right out of nursing school I got this really great job working at a hospital in my hometown. I've always been passionate about helping others and I just knew this was going to be the career I had for the rest of my life.

Most new nurses in this place typically start on the night shift and I was no different. I was thrown into the fire right off the bat by being stationed on one of the hardest floors. The Cancer Ward. Although it is amazing to see people overcome such a terrible illness, it is a fact of the job that not everyone is successful in beating it.

Other than the ER, in my hospital this ward sees more death than any other because of the severity of cases that come through here. The patients become like a part of your family and when one of them doesn't pull through it is always a tough thing to deal with.

When someone dies, two people are assigned to take the body down to the morgue. This room in small given the size of the building we're in and is very cramped. Even during the day it is a little creepy being in there and at night it reaches another level.

One particular evening me and one of my friends were taking a body downstairs and were chatting a bit trying to keep our minds off the grizzly task. We wheeled the remains into the freezer and started finishing up the paperwork for the transfer. Out of nowhere I heard a voice from inside the cold storage begin screaming for help.

Just as quickly as it started the room went quiet.

Every part of my body was shaking. I've never been more terrified in my life. I looked over to my friend and I saw a look that probably resembled the one on my face: Wide eyes, mouth open, basically scared as hell considering the only thing on the other side of the door was the body, we both had just wheeled in there.

It was her that finally found her voice first. "Did you just hear that?"

"Yeah, do you think we should check to see if someone is in there?" I asked her. I reached my hand out for the handle getting ready to open up the freezer despite my better judgement.

"Hell no! Are you crazy?" she told me as she slapped my hand.

I was so relieved to hear that she didn't want to open up the door and see what was causing the noise. Instead, we finished our paperwork and basically ran our way to the elevator as quickly as we could. By the time we were back on our floor I had finally managed to get control of the panic that had taken hold of me.

It probably wasn't the best idea but the two of us went to our supervisor and told her what we'd heard. Her reaction wasn't what either of us had expected. She just smiled at us and said we weren't the only ones who'd experienced something strange down there. I was surprised this was the case since nobody had mentioned anything to me before. This is just the kind of story that I'd have thought everyone would know about given its nature.

When I think about it, I suppose it only makes sense that a place like this that has so much pain and at times death would contain the spirits of some of those that have passed on.

After that night the two of us started another tradition that a lot of the other staff had adopted themselves. Every time somebody dies on our floor, we open the window so that their spirit has a way to escape and isn't trapped with the body. I know that may sound kind of silly but since we started doing that, we haven't experienced anything like we did that night.

To this day I hate going down to that room and I refuse to do so by myself if at all possible. Despite the fact that nothing has happened so far, doesn't mean I want to tempt fate into proving me wrong.

CHAPTER

4

A Chance To Say Goodbye

Just over ten years ago my mother lost her fight with cancer. It was the third time it had returned and from the very beginning she knew this time it was going to get the better of her. After this realization she went downhill very quickly, whether that was from her giving up the fight or the aggressiveness of the cancer I don't know. Either way, within six months of the diagnosis she was gone.

On the day she died I had booked a plane to Arizona where she was living because my sister told me that the doctors had said it was time to say goodbye. "You need to hurry." is what she told me. I booked my flight for the next day and hoped that my mother would be able to hold on long enough for me to get there.

As soon as the plane touched down in Phoenix, I turned on my phone and a chorus of alerts told me that I had missed a number of text messages and voice mails. It took me only a few seconds to realize what had happened. Mom was gone, and worse yet, I was too late.

When I arrived at the hospital I was directed to a Family Room where a pastor was speaking to the members of my family. From the few words I heard before he paused I could tell he was just wrapping up what he was saying. Maybe it was my own emotions for not having a chance to say goodbye but I swear there was a look of disappointment on his face.

The rest of my family was a different story. They all turned towards me in unison, and I could see pain. The scab that had just began to form over the fresh wound would have to be torn off in order to give me the details of what I'd missed. As much as I wish I could spare them, I had to know what had happened.

My dad excused himself from the room and led me to an empty part of the waiting room where we could have some relative privacy. I could tell he was trying to keep it together for me but he was hanging on by a thread. That thread snapped in him and me when he told me my mom had been asking where I was just before she died.

There was nothing else he could have said that could have caused more pain than that. I think he was trying to tell me my mom was thinking of me and loved me right up until the moment she died. Instead, it filled my heart with regret, for not spending more time with her while she still had some life in her but mostly for not being here because I prioritized a project at work instead of leaving immediately. I never felt like more of a failure as a daughter than that moment.

That is when a man in blue scrubs began to wave at me as if he wanted to speak to me over by a set of swinging doors. I told my dad I would be right back and walked over to see what he could want.

I remember vividly he asked me, "I know you weren't here when she died so I was wondering if you'd like me to take you down to the morgue so you could say goodbye to your mother."

The kindness this nurse was showing me overwhelmed what control I had over my emotions and tears bubbled up and overflowed down my cheeks. I was too touched to talk and all I could manage was a weak nod.

He led me through the doors to an elevator where he pressed the down arrow. It arrived with a light *ding* and we both stepped in. He pressed the button that was labeled B2, and the doors closed.

The nurse or doctor, I'm not sure what he was remained quiet for the short ride down and only spoke when we stepped out into a cold white hallway. "Follow me."

We took a couple of turns down side passages

before arriving at a large nondescript door that had a placard telling me that it was the morgue. I'd never been in one of these places before so I didn't really know what to expect other than what I'd seen on television and movies.

The reality was it was an empty tiled room with a large stainless steel wall that had a number of drawers that I guessed held the bodies of those who'd died. It smelled like most other parts of the hospital except the cleaner scent was stronger. Another wall had a counter with cupboards above and below. Off to one side there was a gurney and based on the shape of the sheet on top of it, there was a body still on it.

I looked over to the man and he nodded in the direction of the bed. I felt him place his hand on my shoulder and whisper in my ear, "I'll give you a few minutes, take your time. I believe she'll hear you."

The last part was an odd thing to say but it hit the right note in my heart. I wanted her to know that she was important to me, and I loved her. No, I needed her to know that and this was my chance to tell her.

I took a deep breath trying to steady my nerves and walked over. I took hold of the sheet, all it would take was a quick move and I would see my mom's body, but it was like my hands froze. I tried to tell myself I wanted this but nothing I did allowed me to move that sheet. I let go with a huff of breath and realized what the man had meant. *She can hear you...*

The body under the sheet, although my mom at one point in time wasn't her any longer. The part that made her my mom was gone now and I could speak to her at any point in time. I just had to open my heart to it.

The floodgates on my eyes let go and I bawled as I poured my heart out to her spirit, telling her how much I love her, and I would never forget her. I told her I was sorry I didn't make it in time and I hoped she would forgive me and I shared with her some of the best memories we shared as I grew up and grew into an adult. It was such a liberating and moving experience by the time I was done I was sure my mom had heard me, I was so full of love.

When I got back to the waiting room I saw my dad was sitting in a chair not far from where I'd left him before I left. I told him I'd been taken down to the morgue so I could say goodbye to mom and I wanted to thank whoever the man was who'd taken me down.

His face scrunched up in a look of confusion. "What man are you talking about?" he asked me.

"You know, the guy in the blue scrubs standing by the door that waved me over when we were talking."

That is when he told me that I'd left on my own. He'd seen me walk through the doors to the inner part of the hospital but there hadn't been anyone with me. He'd figured I just needed some time to process what had happened and went for a walk.

I insisted that there was a man that had taken me down there, but my dad wouldn't budge. To prove my point I went over to the information desk and asked if there was a doctor or nurse that matched the description of the one who'd taken me down there. They said there could have been a lot of people who'd fit the description but I couldn't give them enough details to be sure but I was told they hadn't seen anyone wearing blue scrubs anywhere in the vicinity for a while.

To this day I'm not really sure what to believe. Was there really a doctor or nurse that had taken me down to the morgue to say goodbye to my mom or was this some sort of spirit or angel that was sent to me so I could get some closure and relief in a moment where was experiencing great pain. To this day my dad insists that there wasn't anyone there. Spirit, angel or good Samaritan, I thank them for what they did that day.

CHAPTER

5

The Marks

As strange as it may sound, I always wanted my job. You see, I work in a morgue. Sure, it's a job a lot of people would have a really hard time with. Working with dead people isn't for everyone. For me though, I enjoy a puzzle and there is no puzzle more complex than the human body. Trying to come up with the reason why it stops working is a challenge and one that I've dedicated my life to solving.

Despite this, there was a series of events that happened over a week period that nearly pushed me to leave my profession entirely. During this time, I was the only person doing autopsies and I had a number of cases that I'd yet to finish.

In order to keep the rate of decomposition low, the corpses are placed into a refrigerated drawer. One particular morning I walked in to find what appeared to be finger marks all over and around the stainless steel drawers where the bodies are stored.

At first I didn't really think that much about it since there could have been any number of reasons why a person might come in to check one of the bodies. Even though it is policy to always wear protective gloves while doing so in order to protect you and keep from contaminating the body itself, this isn't always followed if there is no intention of touching anything or out of sheer carelessness. I prefer my work area to be neat so I took the time to clean up the streaks and went about my day.

The next morning I came back to find the exact same thing happened again. This time though the streaks were longer and covered much more of the stainless steel surface. At this point I knew this was intentional. Either someone was playing a trick on me, or they just really didn't like me enough to do this.

The latter didn't make any sense because I didn't know of anyone who would maliciously do this. But after taking the half hour to clean up the mess I was determined to figure out who was the culprit.

When the day was over I made a point to turn on the digital video camera that I use to record the autopsies towards the refrigerator in hopes that the person would come back again that night and repeat their twilight antics. The memory on the camera was more than enough to last the entire night so I was confident I would know by morning who was at fault.

When I came in the next day I was horrified by the scene I saw. Nearly every inch was covered by streaks. It would take hours for me to properly clean it, time that I couldn't afford being the only one down here at the time. Still, I was happy to see the camera was still on and had in my estimation captured the entire thing.

I booted up my computer and plugged in the SD card to review the footage. I scanned through hours of footage looking for someone to walk in. About five hours into the recording, I began to see the streaks appear but to my surprise I'd somehow missed the person come in.

I quickly rewound the recording to just before the point where the streaks started and played it at regular speed. What I saw on there was both surprising and upsetting. Nobody walked into the morgue, but the streaks just seemed to appear on their own.

It wasn't until I took a closer look that I saw something that I'd never expected. Orbs. Three of them in fact seemed to swirl in the area right in front of the refrigerator. As they did so it looked as if the streaks themselves would follow.

Frankly I didn't really know what I was looking at. For all intents and purposes there wasn't any way to explain what I was seeing. I've always been a person who was a believer in the paranormal, but even that being the case I didn't want to accept that was what was happening here.

Again I rewound the footage to the point where the orbs first appeared. Low and behold they seemed to emerge from three drawers that were right next to one another. Sadness seemed to flow through me as I recalled the bodies of the people in them. Earlier in the week a drunk driver had crossed the median and hit a car carrying a mother and her three kids head on. The mom had died on impact, but the three children had lingered for a few hours at the hospital before passing away.

Cases involving children were always hard since I had a daughter of my own. The autopsies were one's that I'd been putting off since it would be a painful. They were far too young to lose their lives.

The video clearly showed the orbs came from where the bodies of the three children were. I had no real proof it was the spirits of the kids that were doing this, but something about it just felt right. It just felt like something a child would do. I figured the only way for it to stop would be to complete the examination, painful as it might be.

This proved to be the last night in which the marks showed up. I'm not sure if that is because they were being acknowledged or some other reason. This singular moment was one that had me questioning if I was doing the right thing with my degree. *Maybe I should be trying to save lives rather than figure out what ended them.* In the end, I decided to stay.

CHAPTER

6

Scratching

After graduating from medical school I was already starting to realize the dream of becoming a doctor wasn't even close to how television had portrayed it. Although I had gotten good grades, I wasn't one of the top students in my graduating class. This meant there wasn't a bunch of hospitals lining up to hire me. Mountains of student debt were coming due and I was bound and determined not to move back into my parent's home.

It didn't take me long before I began applying for jobs I would still have a use for my degree, but wasn't something that most people in my position would be seeking out. One such job was working in the morgue at one of my local hospitals. The job would entail doing routine checks for cause of death but mostly it would consist of doing the paperwork for releasing bodies to various locations.

Was it glamorous? Absolutely not. But it was a job, and I needed a way to pay the bills. Besides, I thought, it gave me a foot in the door. Once I proved myself to be more than just my college transcripts, I would have an opportunity to apply for positions that came open.

Like most rooms of its type, the morgue was located in the basement of the hospital. This meant no natural light and little to no visitors unless a body was being dropped off or picked up. It was definitely a job for someone who liked their time alone. The one saving grace, or so I thought, was my shift was during the daytime.

A few months after I had started I was just finishing up a transfer when I began to hear a scratching noise coming from behind one of the doors where we store the bodies. The first thought that went through my head was there a rat that had chewed its way in and had gotten trapped inside.

As I neared the door, the scratching seemed to get louder, more insistent. The image my mind conjured of the rodent making a meal of the deceased inside had my stomach turning, but there wasn't any way I could just ignore it. I made my steps loud enough in hopes that whatever was inside would go quiet but that wasn't the case.

When I pressed my ear to the drawer I could feel what felt like vibrations coming from the other side.

It's more scared of you than you are of it. I tried to tell myself this over and over again, but I knew that probably wasn't true.

I was convinced that once I opened the door the rat would jump out at me so I decided to just open the hatch as quickly as I could. My heart was racing in my chest even before I took hold of the handle. I scrubbed the picture of the rat chewing on the corpse from my brain and flung it open.

Metal contacted metal with a loud *crack* as the door rebounded back but did not latch.

Nothing immediately happened and I found the courage to reach out and start cracking the door open wider an inch at a time. It took nearly a full minute before I could see inside the drawer.

I pulled the sliding table all the way out so I could see the full extent of the damage. Instead of the expected mess, the shroud over the body was undisturbed and after pulling it back, nothing seemed to be out of the ordinary. I took out the small LED light in my desk and shined it to the back of the drawer but the space was empty.

No rat. No hole. Nothing.

The whole thing had me stumped. Even though I was convinced I had opened the right drawer I proceeded to inspect every other compartment just to be sure. Like the first, there didn't seem to be any sign of the furry culprit.

The other guy who worked their full time was a doctor by the name of Stanley Parker. Five days a week we would see each other while passing off any relevant information and happenings that went on during our shift. Although he worked the overnight shift, Staley wasn't your typical morgue doc. He was young, had a great sense of humor and was always willing to talk.

I figured he would know something about what had happened but when I asked him about it I should have known exactly what his response was going to be. He burst out laughing, and told me that I had watched far too many movies about creepy things happening in morgues.

"It's probably just a vibration in the cooling unit," he told me.

His reasoning was sound. It was far more likely it was something mechanical rather than a more insidious cause so I laughed it off as that being the case and put it out of my mind thinking this was a one off.

The problem was, it wasn't. Before long it was happening more days than it didn't. Not only that it never seemed to come from the same place. Even if there wasn't a body in the drawer it didn't preclude it from being the source of the noise.

Finally I had had enough and I called Building Maintenance to come and check out the issue. I told him what had been going on and he gave me a look like I one of those guys who were scared of their own shadow. Still, he took an hour looking over the cooling unit before informing me there wasn't anything wrong with it.

I wasn't surprised at his answer, but I was really hoping to be mistaken, especially in this case. With no mechanical issue and no sign of an animal getting into it I was at a loss for an explanation. In the back of my mind the word *ghost* kept fighting its way to the surface, but I was a man who didn't believe in that kind of thing.

The scratching noises continued for as long as I worked there. Fortunately I received a job at another hospital allowing me to leave. To this day I'm not sure what caused those noises and as far as I knew there wasn't any other reports of strange things happening since. Part of me is still curious as to what was going on in those lockers, but some questions are better left alone.

CHAPTER

7

Creepy Crawly

One of the worst parts of working in a hospital is when a person dies. This is especially the case when it is one of the patients that you have gotten close to. Death can be a regular thing for someone like myself who works in the cancer wing. You will see people of all ages dealing with this horrible disease who and can spend months watching the go through one of the worst experiences of their lives as they try and fight back.

Unfortunately not all of them win. When this

happens one of the worst parts of my job is to take the person's body down to the morgue. And after what happened to me one night, the lines I thought existed between the living and the dead changed forever.

I looked down at the face that just a few hours ago was contorted in unimaginable pain as her body fought shutting down. I know she was scared to die, she'd told me as such, but she had accepted it and had a chance to say goodbye to the ones that were most important to her. It is still amazing to me how many people that are about to cross over are the ones who are comforting those that they will leave behind. But now her fight is done and the pain she was experiencing is in the past.

I lift the white sheet over her and maneuver around to the end of the gurney. As I push the cart down the hall, I see people looking at me out of the corner of their eyes. It isn't just the patients or their families but the staff too. Susan had been here for three weeks as her body slowly failed her.

She had been here multiple times before, whether that be for chemo or any other therapy in a desperate attempt to save her life, only to go home again. In the end, none if it had worked though and the people in the wing would miss her. She was the woman everyone said would beat this because she was fighting so hard but that just didn't happen.

I reached the elevator and Tish, the woman going down with me, hit the down button. It takes only a few seconds before the chime announces the car's arrival. The doors open and I see a few people filing out onto the floor All of them give the bed a wide berth as if the woman beneath the sheet carries some sort of deadly disease.

It is funny how superstitious people are around here. Hospitals are dedicated to treating the sick and wounded and when we fail the ones who are charged with doing so can take it the hardest. Some doctors refuse to even be around a dead person thinking that somehow death carries with it jinx.

I push Susan in, and Tish hits the button for the basement. The elevator jumps to life and begins its decent into the bowels of the building. The bed rattles from the jostling of the sudden movement and I grip the handles a little tighter to make sure it doesn't roll around. I watch the numbers on the red LED panel reduce until the letter B is displayed. I hear the chime again and the door slide open to a long white hallway.

Tish walks out first and I start to push the bed out behind her. Suddenly the lights in the elevator flicker and when I'm about halfway out, the doors begin to close. The surprise causes me to pull my hands back and all I can do is watch as both collide with the gurney at nearly the same time. Luckily the sensor inside the doors pops them open again without damaging the elevator or the bed itself.

"That was weird," I tell Tish.

"Yeah, this place down here gives me the creeps," she says in response.

I grab the handles again and push the bed

through the rest of the way, this time without any further problems. Our footsteps echo through the empty hall as the entrance to our destination comes into view. Tish doesn't fail to remind me that she was the one who put the body in the last time we came down here so it was my turn to do it.

"Great, I get to push the bed and put her away, it must be my lucky day," I reply with an obvious fake smile.

To get to the morgue you have to push the body up a ramp before you get to the large swinging metal door. I lean into the bed and push a little harder to make it up the incline. Tish and I set the brakes on the wheels, and I grab the large handle on the door and pull.

The door makes a slight popping noise as it opens as the rubber seal is broken. The room itself is fairly small and the first thing you notice is the smell. Despite the cold temperatures it is still terrible, formaldehyde and slow decay. It is a good thing I haven't eaten anything recently because the stench is especially vile today.

I push the bed all the way to the back where a loud {thunk} tells me I've hit the back wall. The cold inside the room sends goosebumps up and down my arms as turn to leave. At this point I want nothing more than to get out of here. As I go to walk out the large steel door swings shut encasing me in the freezing cold.

"Tish! This isn't funny! Let me out!" I yell through the door.

The lights flicker and half of them go out. I reach over to toggle the switch off then on again, but the dead bulbs refuse to illuminate. I bang on the door with my fist hoping Tish gets the clue that I'm anything but amused with this and I want to be let out. I hear a muffled voice on the other side of the door but am unable to make out what it is she's saying.

A clicking noise comes from behind me. I look up to the fan in the vent thinking it's the source of the noise but the fan isn't moving.

"Huh, that's weird..." I say to the empty room.

Suddenly it feels like the already freezing temperature drops at least 10 more degrees. The tapping noise begins to get louder and more insistent. I look around, trying to find out where it is coming from. It sounds like something striking metal, but the only thing metal in the room is the drawers holding the bodies. The ticking starts again. This time it is most definitely coming from the drawers, but I don't know how that could be. The only thing in there would be the bodies.

I walk over to the drawer in question and put my ear right next to it trying to hear if in fact that was where it was coming from but the ticking refuses to cooperate. I walk back to the door readying to start my protest to Tish all over again. As soon as my open palm hits the door, the entire room goes black. Without light I couldn't see an inch in front of my face so I put my back to the door so I had some idea of where I was at.

I begin to slap the surface behind me over and over again as the dark feels like it is closing in round me.

"Help me, please help me," a raspy female voice says in front of me.

I panic and begin to scream. "Tish! Tish, get me out of here!"

Tears of fear and panic sting my eyes and face as they trickle down my cold cheeks. Someone or something is in here with me and I am almost thankful I can't see what is talking to me. I hear a dragging noise coming towards me on the floor and I feel something touch my foot.

I recoil onto one leg trying to get away from what must be right beneath me. "Tish! Please!" I sob.

The unseen thing grabs hold of my leg, and I feel like it's pulling itself up my body. I slap my hand again and again on the door trying to get her to open it.

When something touches the area near my stomach, I clench my eyes shut hoping to shut any vision of the phantom in front of me The next thing I know I'm falling backwards. I'm weightless for a moment then pain explodes in my head as it contacts the concrete floor.

At first I am sure that whatever was on me has pulled me to the ground, but hear Tish's voice above me. "Hey, are you okay? The door wouldn't open, it must have gotten stuck," she says.

I reach up to touch the back of my head and feel the beginnings of a nasty bump where I'd knocked it when I'd fallen. My eyes dart to the freezer, looking for signs from whatever had been in there with me but the room is empty and all the lights are on.

I didn't think there was any way I could hallucinate the entire thing, at least I didn't think so, but all that was in the room was the bed I'd just pushed in.

"I need to get out of here now," I tell her.

She looks at me with an openly confused look. "What are you talking about?"

"I need to get out of here now," I say with a little more force.

She cocks an eyebrow up at me then turns and shuts the door. "You're acting weird." She reaches up towards my face. "Let me look at your head."

"I'm fine, let's just go, please." I shoo her off with a hand.

It takes everything I have not to run straight for the elevator that night. But I can tell you the sense of relief I felt when I got back to our floor was such that it was like a huge weight had been lifted off my chest. I will not go down there alone to this day. I found out later that I'm not the only one who's had experiences down there, but until that night I wouldn't have believed them if they'd told me. These days, I try to pass off the duty any time I can. So far, I've had no other experiences down there, I just hope it stays that way.

CHAPTER

8

Extreme Contact

During the early 70's while I was growing up my grandfather was the caretaker of a local cemetery. It was always a subject that my friends found interesting, especially around Halloween. Every year we would stay up as late as we could roving around the grounds hoping to spot a ghost or other supernatural entity. In all the time we did this, nothing that went bump in the night ever appeared outside. Inside the building however is another story.

Burned out from our late night excursions that

amounted to what we considered a giant waste of time, me and my four friends decided to change things up a bit. That Halloween we were given permission to stay the night in the morgue where the bodies were prepared and stored before the services. It took a lot of begging on my part, but in the end he relented only because there wasn't any remains being stored at the time.

The five of us arrived around 9:00, sleeping bags in hand. Other than a cooler full of snacks and drinks my friend Jeff brought with him another item that he'd borrowed from his sister. A Ouija board. Immediately I thought it was a great idea considering our previous failures, but Marshal and Todd weren't so sure. We'd already had to basically pressure them to show up that night. Adding the board I'm sure felt like we were twisting the knife a bit.

In the end all five of us stayed. The night itself started off like most others. We talked about the girls we thought were hot and caught each other up on the latest stories we'd heard from around school. Since we saw each other almost every day there wasn't much we didn't know about our lives, but it did put the two who were apprehensive more at ease.

It was about 11:30 when the conversations seemed to die out and it was time for the main event of the evening. At this point I even had to admit I was feeling a bit nervous. Even in the daylight this room was a bit creepy. Now we were here at night with the intention of contacting the spirits who might be trapped here. To put it lightly the idea was becoming less and less appealing, even to me.

We lit a few candles and sat in a circle around the board, waiting for someone to touch the planchette. It was Wade who finally broke the stalemate by placing two fingers on the arrow shaped piece of plastic. When it didn't start sliding all over the board spelling out messages of doom the four of us followed suit.

We followed the instructions that came with the board and announced to the room that we there to listen to any spirits that might want to speak with us. I now know this isn't what you want to say because it also allows for those who might mean you harm to enter as well.

We slid the planchette round in a circle a few times and asked if there were any spirits present. Almost immediately the indicator moved to YES on the board. I look up and Jeff has a huge grin on his face, and I know he'd done it trying to get a rise out of us. I had to admit it was funny but Marshal and Todd didn't find it as amusing.

Jeff wiped off his grin and said he'd take it seriously and spoke out that we were there to communicate. All of us sat there waiting for something to happen but after a couple of minutes of sitting there I was starting to wonder if this was also going to be a bust like all our other Halloweens.

I was just about to say something when it felt like someone blew a gust of air into my ear. The sensation sent a shiver through me and I turned ready to scold Wade for his antics.

"What the hell man? I thought we were taking this seriously."

He turned to me and pulled a face. "I am, you're the one who's talking."

His tone and response immediately had me on the defensive. "You are not, you just blew in my ear."

He was just about to say something when Jeff piped in. "Craig, Wade never moved man. It wasn't him."

I got mad because now two people were telling me what I felt never happened. I started to speak when the planchette slid across the board to the word YES. I looked back to Jeff, but he seemed just as surprised as I did. I looked at the rest of my friends thinking one of them had done it to stop the impending argument but all of them seemed totally fixated on the board.

Todd somehow is the one who could find his voice first and asked if a spirit was in fact present with us. The device moved away from YES before returning a moment later.

All of us were sure it was one of the others doing this but no one would admit to it. Left with little to prove one of us was lying we decided to ask questions about who this supposed spirit was like their name, where they lived and how they had died. All we got were a series of seemingly random letters that didn't make any sense.

Things took a dark turn quickly from there. Without any prompting the planchette began to spell out the word D-I-E over and over again. At first we thought it was telling us they'd died but after the word repeated itself three or four times without stopping we realized we were wrong. After Jeff asked who it wanted to die and we got the response Y-O-U I was more than ready to be finished with the seance.

We went to close it when one of the flames on the candles suddenly went out on its own. This caused the words to die on Jeff's tongue as we all looked at each other no longer believing one of the others had been moving the planchette this entire time. I knew for sure we were in over our heads doing this.

Marshal poked Jeff in the side and he started speaking again closing the circle to the spirits. When he finished, we moved the indicator to GOODBYE. All of us sat in silence but there was a heaviness to the room that hadn't been there when we'd started.

There's a loud knock that comes somewhere behind me and ten eyes point in that direction. With this I've had enough of this place but I'm too scared to move. Every one of us is focused on the area right behind me, terrified of what we might see but more scared of something sneaking up on us.

Marshal screams and twists in the opposite direction of the rest of us. With that the paralysis is broken and my friends and I run for the door abandoning our sleeping bags in our wake.

I'm not sure what we encountered that Halloween night. Despite my mom and dad being unhappy with the state we'd left things the night before it was a full week before I was willing to go back to my grandfather's work to get the things we'd left and even then I refused to touch the Ouija board and I haven't since.

CHAPTER

9

The Pub

Three years ago, I got a job at a pub in my local town. When I told my dad about it, he shared some of the history of the place that he knew, which was actually pretty fascinating to learn about. The pub is situated right next door to the town's police station, and when I worked there it was called 'Whittles', but it used to be called 'The Sergeant at Arms' because of its history as the town's prison.

In the cellar of the pub, there was a blocked-off, cemented wall. Behind that wall is actually a whole underground tunnel system that linked the pub to places all across town, including the police station and some other buildings in the area.

I worked at the pub for just under a year. While I was there, I started dating the son of the pub's owners, who also lived there. He told me about a few experiences he'd had since moving in.

The first night there, he slept in what was to later become the living room. He told me he was shaken awake in the middle of the night, and heard an unfamiliar male voice say: "Go home, this is our place!" There was nobody else around, and he was adamant he hadn't imagined it. That was enough to spook him, and once he had officially moved in, he chose one of the upstairs rooms as his bedroom instead. But that room was just as bad. He had so many strange experiences in there, including doors slamming without reason, hearing someone tapping on the walls, and other odd noises that didn't have any apparent cause. It got to the point where he no longer felt comfortable staying in there and ended up moving into the bedroom next door to that.

When I spent my first night there, I was pretty excited but also a bit nervous about what to expect. I wanted to see if I might experience something paranormal, but at the same time I was too scared to actively seek anything out.

I didn't hear or see anything unusual during that first night, but I did notice that the atmosphere around the pub seemed to change during the early hours of the morning. It was like the whole place just shifted to being suddenly oppressive and unwelcoming, and I got the impression I was being watched from the shadows, even though there was nothing or nobody there. Although I didn't experience anything directly, I did get the sense that something about the place was *off,* though I couldn't quite put my finger on it during that first night.

About four months later, I was finished up a late-night shift at the pub. The pub was closed and the only people inside were the landlords and myself. We were all sitting at the bar, chatting to each other, when I heard the men's toilet door swing open. I was sitting with my back to the door, which was no more than ten feet behind me, so I knew exactly where it had come from. Before I could turn around, I heard someone walk across the wooden floor towards me, accompanied by the sound of jingling keys; it sounded precisely like someone had a ring of keys hooked to their belt, and they were slapping against this person's thigh as they walked.

The footsteps came closer, and as I was turning round to check who it was, I said to my boss, "Who else is in the pub? I thought everyone had gone home?" Before I'd even finished the sentence, I realized there was nobody behind me. Yet I was certain I'd heard the door open a second before, and the sound of footsteps coming towards me.

I seemed to be the only one who found it odd, so I asked my boss if he'd heard the same thing, but he merely joked that I'd drank too much and was imagining things. I was a little bit tipsy but still rational, and I knew what I'd heard. It had been too loud and sounded too close for me to have been mistaken, and yet nobody else had heard it! That was my first 'proper' encounter with the paranormal while I was working at the pub, but it wasn't the last. I was starting to realize at this point that my boyfriend's anxieties about the place weren't unfounded, and there was definitely something going on there.

Another time, I was sitting in my boyfriend's room. It was late in the evening, and we were just chilling on his bed and listening to some music, since he didn't have a television. I remember him telling me that the room felt strange to him, and he got the eerie feeling that something was going to happen. I figured he might have just been a little on edge and thought nothing of it. A short while later, he got up to go to the toilet, so I paused the music and waited alone on his bed.

While he was gone, I started to get a similarly 'eerie' feeling, like I suddenly wasn't alone in the room anymore, even though my boyfriend was still in the toilet. I looked around but couldn't see anything. And then I heard something that made me freeze; from the middle of the bedroom, I heard a very loud, menacing growl. It shocked me but didn't frighten me at the time in the way that it probably should have. It was only looking back on it that I realized I probably should have been more freaked out, especially knowing that demonic entities were known to growl like that. My boyfriend came back from the toilet, but I didn't mention what I'd heard as I didn't want to freak him out more than he already was.

Later that same night, we both got hungry and headed downstairs to get some crisps. The cellar to the pub was locked, as it always was when it wasn't being used, and we had to walk past it to get to the small kitchen area where the food was kept. Just as we passed it, we heard a noise coming from inside. It sounded like rustling, as though someone was crinkling a packet of crisps together. It was very strange, and neither of us knew what could have been making such a noise. We exchanged a puzzled glance but decided to ignore it since the cellar was locked. We hurried grabbed our snacks from the kitchen and started to walk back upstairs. We'd barely made it to the third step when we heard a huge thud come from inside the cellar, followed by more crinkling and rustling, as though someone had knocked a full box of crisps over. We both froze and listened, but the last straw was when something started to knock heavily against the door. The two of us bolted up the stairs, too scared to open the cellar door and check it out.

    About a week after the incident in the cellar, my boyfriend, his mum and I were all sitting in the kitchen. The kitchen was connected to a long corridor which led to the downstairs area of the pub, and the main entrance. While we were all talking, we heard footsteps running down the corridor, and what sounded like a child's giggle. My boyfriend had a three-year-old niece called Ellie who often liked to visit, and although she wasn't due to visit that day, we assumed she'd come as a surprise. We all stood up, saying "Aww, Ellie's here!" and went out to greet her. But when we stepped out into the hallway, there was nobody there. The pub below was empty too, and there were no other children present in the pub. We were all pretty freaked out, since all three of us had clearly heard the footsteps and the giggle, so nobody had been imagining it.

The weirdest experience I had at the pub happened when my boyfriend's parents decided to go on holiday. They had asked me to stay in the pub for the week and keep the upstairs flat safe while they were away. I had just finished my shift at the pub and was heading upstairs to the flat. I decided to phone my boyfriend just as I was opening the door to the flat to ask him what he wanted cooking for tea. While we were talking, I was trying to unlock the door, but for some reason it just wouldn't turn. I tried for a solid two minutes to get into the flat, but I couldn't seem to disengage the lock. I eventually told my boyfriend that I couldn't get inside, but he just laughed at me and said, "Maybe the ghosts don't want you there!" Almost as soon as he said that the phone signal went completely haywire. We both heard about twenty different voices coming through the line, all speaking at once, and none of which were understandable. I remember noticing that a lot of the voices sounded panicked and distressed, though I could never pick up on what they were saying.

I finally managed to turn the key in the lock and get the door open, and as soon as I stepped into the flat, the voices stopped. I was still connected to the call to my boyfriend, but the two of us were stunned into silence. Neither of us knew what we'd just heard, so we decided to hang up and talk about it later, when he was back home from work.

The next hour of sitting alone in the flat, waiting for him to come back from work, was probably one of the most unsettling I'd had. The call had really freaked me out. I knew it was probably just a bad signal and we'd somehow crossed wires, but it didn't feel that way, especially given all of the other strange experiences I'd had here.

There were many other things that happened during the time I worked there. Sometimes I'd hear something rapping on the walls, like they were trying to get my attention, and I had things fall randomly from shelves on occasion, even when there was no probable cause. I always tried to figure out if there was a rational explanation for these occurrences, but most of the time there wasn't. Eventually I got used to things happening, and it stopped bothering me after a while. I once asked the owners if they had ever considered holding some kind of séance there, just to see what they picked up, but they refused. They were the ones who had to live there, after all, and they'd rather not go stirring up things that were best left alone.

CHAPTER

10

Pray

A few years ago, my ex-husband and I moved to Pretoria. He'd got a new job working as a prison guard at Pretoria Prison, so it had been easier to move there than travel. While we were waiting for his employer to supply us with accommodation, we stayed at my aunt's house. She didn't mind, and I think she enjoyed it since she was living alone in her old, big house, so our company was a welcome change. The house itself was old, but I didn't feel anything particularly strange there, except for the room my husband and I stayed in. Whenever I walked in, I always got the feeling that someone was watching me. It's hard to explain, but it just felt like I wasn't alone in there, even when I was. It didn't bother me too much, though, so I tried to ignore it.

My son was about one year old at that time. One night, he started acting strange. He kept pointing his finger to the wall and ceiling above where his bed was, like he was trying to show me something, but there was nothing there that I could see. He kept saying 'mamma, mamma' and pointing desperately at the wall; by his expression alone, I knew he wasn't just pretending. There was something there that I couldn't see, and it was distressing him. I was confused but not scared at that time. I took him out of his bed and calmed him down, and eventually he fell back asleep, but I never knew what he'd seen.

Another night while staying in that room, I woke up to something sitting on my feet. I thought it was the cat sleeping at the bottom of the bed, since he did that sometimes. I always slept on my stomach, so I had to twist my body around to see it, but the cat was so heavy it was hard to move, and I couldn't really see it in the darkness of the room. Since it was keeping me awake, I tried to kick the cat off.

Kicking it was the last thing I should have done. Because the thing sitting on my feet wasn't a cat at all.

The thing moved off my legs, but then I felt a crushing pressure around my throat, like someone had wrapped their hands around it and was trying to strangle me. The fact that there was nobody there was what made me realise that what I'd kicked was a *ghost*. And it wasn't happy.

I started to pray, desperate for the ghost to leave me alone. After repeating the prayer three times, it finally disappeared, and I could breathe again. I immediately jumped out of bed and switched on the light. My son was awake too, and once again he was pointing his finger above him in the same place as before, even though there was nothing there. My ex finally woke up at that point, but he wasn't sensitive to these things, so he had no idea what was going on.

That wasn't the last of the encounters, though.

The room in which we were staying was along a long hallway that connected to a bathroom as well as the sitting room. I was busy brushing my teeth in the bathroom one evening when something caught the corner of my eye.

I turned my head to look down the hallway and was surprised to see a face staring back. It was a man whom I didn't recognise, peering around the edge of the doorway, almost as though he was checking to see if the hallway was clear before entering it. When he saw me, he looked just as taken aback as I was, as though he was shocked that I was able to see him.

I didn't realise at first, but there was something dramatically wrong with his appearance. His skin was grey and almost translucent, like I was looking at him through a watery film. He was an older man with grey hair and a lined face, though it was difficult to make out the details because of his oddly blurry appearance.

He quickly backed into the sitting room, and I followed after him, thinking he might be an intruder. But when I looked into the room, there was nobody there. The only exit was through that doorway, so there was no way else he could have gone.

I never saw that man again, but I didn't forget his face.

While this was happening, I never told my aunt any of it. I didn't want to upset her, especially since this was happening in her house.

I figured that if they didn't disturb her, then there was no need to make her worry needlessly.

A few days after seeing the ghost, I was sitting with my aunt and going through some old photo albums of hers. When she showed me some photos from when she was younger, I recognised one of the men in the picture. It was the ghost I'd seen in the hallway. I immediately asked her who he was, and she told me that it was her husband. He died a long time ago, and I'd been too young at the time to remember him. I wouldn't have recognised him at all if I hadn't seen him only a few days prior.

We eventually moved into new accommodation, leaving my aunt alone in that big house, but she never mentioned anything strange.

It's strange that ghosts seem to be able to hide themselves from us, for the most part. I don't know what caused me to have all these experiences while my husband and aunt didn't. But one thing I'm certain of is that I'll never kick a ghost again.

CHAPTER

11

Historic

My husband and I decided to revisit a very beautiful town called Blairsville. It's a very small, simple little place with limited attractions, but a very full history. It's completely surrounded by the Georgia mountains, and full of old-fashioned Southern hospitality. I was nine-months pregnant at the time, and since I was due to be induced soon, and my husband had some time off, we thought it was a good idea to go sightseeing. Blairsville was fairly close to where we lived, so that's where we headed.

In the center of the town square was Blairsville's historic courthouse, which had been built in 1899. The courthouse had to undergo some repairs during the 1920s due to a lack of preservation, but the changes were minimal at best, and it was placed on the national register of historic places in 1980.

It stands beautifully in the middle of a small, grassy lot, and is built mainly of brick with a tall white clock- and belltower. On the lawn to the side of the building, encased in a glass box, is one of the original bells.

The building itself comprises two floors, the first being where the museum is. As soon as we walked in, we were greeted by a kind, older woman who welcomed us to the courthouse. The floors were made of some kind of cherry hardwood, and the walls were full of displays; old farming equipment with black and white photos of fields, crops and the farmers working them; folded flags; old advertisements and newspaper clippings in frames.

The first room was rather small, containing an old school desk, a sewing mannequin wearing a simple flower-patterned dress, and a glass case filled with various miscellaneous items; thimbles and old buttons, postage stamps, coins, a pair of women's laced gloves, teacups and plates. There were also pictures of schoolchildren and families, and lots of the town itself. It's definitely a place rich with history, so I recommend paying a visit if you like that sort of stuff.

The second room was much more intense in terms of the atmosphere. For some reason, when I'm around older items, I tend to be sensitive to certain emotions lingering around them, such as those that belonged to the original owner.

Since the second room was filled with war items, the atmosphere was much heavier. There were all sorts of uniforms, bullets, guns and swords, letters and medals on display. As soon as I walked in, I almost walked back out again. The whole place was brimming with feelings of sadness, anger and fear. As I walked around the room, I began to feel, hear and see the remnants attached to the objects. I could smell the gunpowder, the sweat and blood and dirt buried into the fabric of the uniforms. I could hear the echoes of screams and shouts, and very faintly, the sound of gunfire. When I began to feel a shooting pain in my chest, I decided it was best to get out of the room as quickly as possible, before the feelings got worse.

I think I must have been experiencing someone else's final moments. Or perhaps, because of the abundance of artefacts in the room, it was a flood of different memories washing over me at once, making me feel all these different things. Either way, it was making me feel really uneasy, so I stepped out into the hall and waited for my husband to finish looking around.

When he was done, we headed up to the second floor, which was the old courtroom. It was now used for small gatherings, and there were sometimes events held here, including a place for kids to take photos with Santa during the holidays. When we went, there was nothing on, so it was fairly empty.

It was a rather large room, capable of holding around 70-100 people somewhat comfortably. There was still a judge's bench, as well as witness stands on either side. All of it was roped off, but the rest of the room was filled with pews. The walls themselves were lined with old windows that still had their original panes, and some old photographs of the courtroom when it was still being used for cases.

As I walked around the room, I noticed an unsettling presence around me, almost as though I was being watched from the shadows. I took a look around, but my husband and I were the only ones in the room. I stuck close to him, trying to shake away the feeling of unease.

We were standing still, looking at some of the old black-and-white photographs, when I felt two hands firmly grip my hips from behind. It was a very sudden, aggressive motion, and all the hairs on my neck stood on end as a cold gust of wind blew down my back.

It was then that I heard a deep male voice whisper in my ear: "Guilty. I was guilty and freed."

That was the last straw for me. I no longer felt comfortable staying there. I asked my husband if we could leave, and for a second, the hands on my hips tightened, as though preventing me from going. But then they let go, thankfully. My husband gave me a funny look and asked if I was okay. I told him I just felt a little fatigued, so the two of us left. Just before I reached the steps, I heard the same voice as before whisper, "fools". I didn't even bother looking back, but just kept walking, eager to get out of there.

I had no idea what he had been guilty of, but even now, I'd rather not find out.

CHAPTER

12

Whispers Between The Drawers

I work as the night janitor at a large hospital. Most of my job is pretty much what you'd expect it to be, but it is how I support myself and my family. Is it glamorous? No, but it's a paycheck.

One of the most common questions I get from people when I tell people what my job is typically is this: *Has anything creepy happened to you there?* I don't know why but people seem to have this obsession with the paranormal. Yes, people die in hospitals and I'm a firm believer in the idea that a person's spirit can linger on if the circumstances are right. I've always believed this though, but this was, at least in my mind, confirmed one evening about six years ago.

I was mopping one of many hallways I'd be visiting that night when I got a call over my radio from the night supervisor telling me that there was a spill that he'd been told needed cleaning up in the basement and if I'd be willing to go take care of it. I told him yes, after which he let me know that it was in the hospital's morgue.

My stomach sank. The least he could have done would have been to tell me where it was before sending me there. It wouldn't be the first time I'd been called down to clean something up, it's not like it was I didn't see on the other floors. The problem was the room just flat creeped me out, especially when I was alone. I had already told my boss I would go though so I grabbed my cart and headed to the basement.

It took me less than five minutes to clean up whatever they'd dropped on the floor. Long ago I had learned it was best not to ask and just get it done as quickly as possible.

A couple hours later I received a similar request which surprised me since there shouldn't have been anyone down there at that time of night to make a mess. I guess it was possible someone had bumped something with a bed but two cleanups in one night in the morgue was almost unheard of.

Again I headed down to the basement and entered the large rectangular room. Almost in the exact same place that I'd mopped up a spill earlier was a similar one. I have to admit I was frustrated with the carelessness of whoever was responsible for these messes but I went to work.

I was just finishing up the last of it when all of the lights in the room suddenly went out. There isn't a window in the door so it was almost completely black. Two possibilities went through my head immediately. First, the hospital had experienced a power outage, or two, someone was messing with me.

When I heard a man and a woman whispering to one another I was almost sure it was the latter possibility. "Hello? Is someone there?" The whispering continued without giving me a response. I tried to figure out what they were saying to each other but it was too quiet to make out any of the words.

I tried to stay calm and spoke to the dark room. "Okay, really funny, mess with the janitor. Can you turn on the lights please?"

But the lights didn't go on and that's when it came to me that the switches were in the opposite direction of where I'd heard the voices. I blindly groped in the dark, hoping to bump into something that would give me an idea where I was at.

I had to move at a snail's pace so it took a while before my hand made contact with something solid. The fact that it was a bare wall did nothing to help me orient myself in the lightless room. I stopped for a second before moving on, but the moment was short lived. The voices seemed to have gotten louder, but the words were no less distinguishable. For some reason this seemed even worse than if I'd been able to make out what they were saying.

I made a decision, something in my head told me I had to go to the right. I began shuttling sideways, brushing my fingers along the unyielding surface, hoping to find something that would tell me where I was. When I was almost certain I'd gone too far my hand bumped painfully against a raised surface. I groped at the object, trying to determine what it was by feel alone.

{A door frame!} The thought alone sent relief coursing through my entire body until I remembered there were two doors in this room. One lead to the hallway, the other was the freezer where the waiting bodies were kept. It was creepy enough just thinking about going in there while being able to see, to do so in the pitch dark, while hearing strange garbled voices wasn't something I wanted to entertain.

Nonetheless I had no choice but to risk that possibility. I reached out and grabbed the knob and twisted. Even in the dark I crushed my eyes shut hoping to shield myself from the view. When no blast of cold air came I opened my eyes enough so that I could squint through the small gap between my eyelids. To my relief it was the hallway.

It was then I realized the voices had gone silent. I quickly turned back and flipped on the lights. Even though the room was empty it didn't do anything to settle the butterflies in my stomach. For once I was really hoping there would have been someone there laughing at my expense.

Even though the lights were on I didn't want to grab my cart. If it were up to me I'd leave the damn thing where it was and hightail it to the elevator. The only reason I did was because I'd be sent back whether I wanted to or not.

That night in the morgue was one of the worst experiences of my life. Now that I think about it, that was probably the moment I decided to transfer to the day shift a few months later. Even so, I always take someone with me when I have to go down there.

CHAPTER

13

Mis-Identification

Ten years ago I received a phone call in the middle of the night. Any parent can tell you when something like that happens their heart feels like it stops for a moment, terrified that something has happened to their baby. I tried to tell myself that he just needed a ride home from a party where he'd been drinking even though he wasn't 21 yet. He would have been in trouble but at least he would have been safe.

When I answered the phone a man immediately introduced himself as a police officer and asked if I was in fact Jason's mother. My mouth felt like it was on autopilot and I told I was. The only words I heard were "I'm sorry..." and the rest just evaporated behind my sobs. I don't know how I got there but the next thing I knew I was curled in the fetal position on the ground.

He told me the hospital had done everything they could but the injuries he sustained when the other car crossed the median were too extensive for them to have saved him. They needed me to come in and verify that it was in fact him that had gotten in the accident.

The entire trip I kept telling myself that I was going to walk into that room and somehow the body of my son wasn't going to be there. I think made every promise I could just for that to be true. I even offered up my own life in exchange.

From the moment I walked into the hospital I started to get a heaviness in my chest, this deep wrongness that continued to build as an officer lead me down a hallway to a windowless door that had a little sign next to it that said MORGUE. He gave me this look as if he expected that I would be the one to open the door. I didn't want to touch the handle though. I'm sure he thought I was in denial that my son was dead and that as long as I didn't go in that room it wasn't real. There was a part of me who believed that, but a voice in the back of my head was telling me to stay away.

The reality was I didn't have much of a choice. Sooner or later I needed to face the truth that lay inside, and as much as I knew it would hurt there was no reason to hold on to false hope. Eventually, he must have realized I was waiting for him to open the door which he did and I stepped in.

The room was much as I had expected. I'd seen places like this on television before, only this time it seemed too plain almost unceremonial for what I was being asked to do. You'd think someone would be brought to a place that put them at ease before maybe seeing their loved one for the last time.

The first thing that I noticed wasn't the bed that had been placed in the middle of the room that had a sheet draped over what was obviously a body. It was like a sixth sense made itself known for the first time. There was a heaviness, almost humid aspect to the air. If the officer hadn't been walking behind me I would have retreated into the hallway and come back in just to see if I was just mistaken.

As I walked further into the room it became oppressive. Not only did it feel like someone was standing right over my shoulder but I was on the verge of being smothered. Five steps is all I took into the room before my feet planted themselves and refused to move. I'm not sure even the officer could have drug me closer if he wanted.

The identification itself was quick. The doctor only removed enough of the drape to show me the face which despite all the promises I'd made turned out to be that of my then-dead son. He was only nineteen years old, and now I as his mother would have to bury him.

I wanted to run from the room but I wanted to maintain a bit of dignity. I believed my son would have wanted me to be strong despite the terrible situation. I thought I owed him at least that.

I left my car at the hospital and called a cab to take me home. I was in no condition to drive, and at the time I'm not sure I ever wanted to leave the safety of my home after I returned, after all, a car was the reason my son was dead.

When I got home sleep was the last thing on my mind. I tried but all I could do was stare at the patterns in the ceiling above my bed. They seemed to blend together recreating the time we spent together from when he was born to when he sat at my dinner table just that morning. At some point, I must have started to cry since my face and pillow were soaked.

I wiped the tears from my eyes when I felt something pressing down on the other side of my bed. I didn't live with anyone at the time and had no pets so the depression of the mattress caught me by surprise. I looked over to where I felt it come from. The spot was sunk lower than the area around it and the comforter was bunched around the edges like it would if someone was sitting there but I was alone in my room.

I am a woman who believes that we all have spirits and that energy passes on when someone dies. However, I think it is possible that a soul or whatever you want to call it can remain for a time if it needs to fulfill some purpose. So when this happened I was sure that my son was here to tell me that he was okay and that he wanted me to know that.

Fresh tears stained my face as they trailed their way down to merge with the blankets. At the time I was so grateful to him for giving me such a gift.

I smiled despite myself and said, "Jason? Is that you?" I sat there for twenty seconds or so, waiting for some sort of response even though for the life of me I'm not sure what I was expecting.

All of a sudden the hairs on the back of my neck stood completely on end and that voice that I'd heard in the hospital that had told me to stay away from the morgue started screaming in my head. {It's not Jason!}

The room suddenly became suffocating and I felt like something crushing me into the bed. I tried to fight but whatever was doing this had me completely overpowered. I tried to buck and twist away but it was like my muscles weren't getting the information from my brain.

It started to hurt to breathe as the effort to expand my chest to get oxygen became immense and then impossible. It was like I was choking on the air itself. When my vision started to tunnel I knew I was in trouble for a few seconds even though I actually thought death was a possibility.

To my surprise, it was over just as quickly as it had started. The pressure just relented allow at once allowing me to take in huge gulps of air. Even so, I was more than shaken, I was terrified. It took a few minutes for my breathing to return to normal and for my heart to not feel like it was trying to rip through the front of my chest.

That was the only time whatever was in my room that night made an appearance. I don't know why it felt the need to do the things it did. Even all these years later I have no doubts that whatever had been in the morgue at the hospital had somehow followed me home and attacked me. I'd let my guard down thinking my son had come home one last time to tell me goodbye. I couldn't have been more wrong.

CHAPTER

14

SARAH

I was seven years old when my family and I moved to a five-bedroomed house on the outskirts of town. Our new neighborhood was in one of the sketchier parts of town, and probably wasn't the most ideal place to raise a family. But my family was big and didn't have a lot of money, so the cheap rent and spacious accommodation were appealing, despite the downfalls of the area.

    The house itself sat on top of a steep hill, with a rickety set of stairs leading up to a porch that had been painted purple by the previous owners. The house was in fairly good condition, albeit with a few cosmetic flaws. From the front door, you ended up straight into the living room, with a direct view of the kitchen and the staircase on the right. From the living room, you could turn left down a hallway, which led down to four of the bedrooms, and a single bathroom.

At the very top of the stairs was a window that overlooked onto the back lawn. To the left on the landing was the fifth bedroom, and to the right was an open area that we used as a second family room. Later on, the whole upstairs section would become my aunt's living quarters when she came to stay with us.

The house, at first, seemed like any other house in that regard. There was a lot of space for my siblings and I, so despite the shady neighborhood, it wasn't a bad place to live. At least, that's what I thought in the first week or so.

But as we settled into the house, it quickly became obvious that we weren't alone there.

The house was being occupied by three spiritual entities during our residence there, and I can recall several instances with each one.

The first entity was an elderly woman who used to sit at the window at the top of the stairs, in the little nook that we used as a storage space. There was also an elderly man who resided in the basement, and a little girl who seemed to be around ten years old. I never really came into contact with the man downstairs, since I very rarely had a reason to go down into the basement. But I had several encounters with the woman at the window, and the little girl especially.

    First I'll tell you about the man in the basement. My mom thought that he had been a previous resident of the house, way back when there used to be plantations here, and that at some point he had a workshop in the basement. This was because the basement usually had a very heavy wood and sawdust smell, like it had been used for woodworking in the past. None of us had any particularly harmful interactions with him, but it was pretty clear that he didn't like people going down to the basement. Whenever anyone went down there, the air would get very heavy and oppressive, and they would be overcome with the feeling that they weren't welcome there.

    I did have a much more personal, and chilling, interaction with the lady at the top of the stairs. The fifth bedroom upstairs had been my playroom until my aunt moved in. One night, I asked my mom if I could sleep over in my playroom instead of my normal bedroom downstairs.

She agreed, so that night, I dragged my sleeping bag upstairs and set it up in the playroom. My mom tucked me in like she always did, and went into the family room just down the hall from me.

As I was lying there, trying to fall asleep, I started to get the weird sensation that I was being watched. My mom had left the door partially open, and I kept staring at the dark gap between the doorframe, expecting someone to be there.

Eventually, I managed to brush it off and started to doze. I hadn't quite managed to fall asleep when I heard a woman's voice call my name. I blinked open my eyes, staring into the darkness, and heard it again. A woman's voice saying, "Hanna, come here baby." Assuming it was my mom, since she was just down the hall from me, I climbed out of my sleeping bag and went to go see what she wanted.

When I asked her why she called me, she looked at me in confusion.

"I didn't call you," she said, everything about her voice and expression sincere.

I told her that I heard her say my name, but she denied it, saying she hadn't said a thing. At this point, I was getting pretty creeped out, because I knew what I'd heard. I ended up going back to my bedroom to sleep, because staying upstairs was too freaky.

My other main paranormal experience in that house happened with a young girl called Sara. She must have been around my age at the time, maybe nine or ten years old, and I used to play with her all the time. I don't remember this myself, but my mom told me that she would see me running around the house and talking to someone who wasn't there, and when she'd ask me what I was doing, I would always reply, "Oh, just playing with Sara." Of course, my mom merely brushed it off as an imaginary friend, since it wasn't uncommon for kids my age to be overly-imaginative. She would later come to realize that wasn't the case at all. Sara was real.

One evening, I was laying on my bed, watching the Disney channel. My TV was at the end of my bed, so I would often lay on my stomach while watching it. At the time, I distinctly remember having my bedroom light on while watching television, because it was getting dark outside and I didn't like the way the TV strained my eyes if I didn't have a light on.

I'm the kind of person who gets super invested when watching TV, and my mind will completely zone out everything else except the show I'm watching.

As soon as the TV went to the commercial break, and my concentration broke, I realized that I was sitting in complete darkness. The light had turned off. With a frown, I climbed off my bed and went to ask who had switched my light off. Of course, my mom and her husband both denied it, and my siblings were too short to reach the switch, so I knew it couldn't have been them. I was certain I would have noticed someone come into my room, and it wasn't like any of them had a reason to turn my light off.

The whole situation was somewhat odd, but I started to suspect that maybe it was Sara messing around with me.

After I told my mom about Sara, even she started to think that perhaps she was more than just an imaginary friend. Imaginary friends couldn't turn lights off, after all.

Eventually we moved out of that house. Once we'd settled elsewhere, though, my mom did some research into the house and the deaths that surrounded it, since my stories of the ghosts living there had obviously piqued her interest.

The most chilling piece of information she discovered was about a little girl called Sara who was killed in a car crash just outside the house. From what we managed to unearth from newspapers and articles at the time, the morgue which Sara's body had been taken to was only a few buildings away from our house. Given the close proximity of the events, it made me wonder if Sara's spirit somehow migrated from the former morgue to our old house.

CHAPTER

15

Discomfort

I was working the late shift at the morgue one night when I got the feeling that I wasn't alone.

As someone who worked with the deceased, I wasn't very open to believing in the paranormal. As far as I was concerned, there was nothing after death. The body died, and that was that.

I'd never been a very paranoid person either, which is why this feeling caught me off guard. It wasn't just my own mind playing tricks on me. It was my body reacting to something that I couldn't see.

All of the hairs on my arms and neck stood on end, and an uneasiness settled in my stomach like a stone, heavy and uncomfortable.

I was in the office, filling out some paperwork before heading home, and I knew I was the only one there. Everyone had already finished for the night. So it didn't make sense why I was suddenly overcome by the feeling that someone – or something – was here in the building with me. We'd had several fresh bodies come in that morning, but that was a regular occurrence and shouldn't have stirred any feelings of paranoia or unease inside me.

I did my best to ignore it, finishing up my work as quickly as I could and locking up behind me.

Even while I was driving home, that feeling of discomfort followed me, and I kept throwing glances up into my rear-view mirror as though expecting someone to be sitting in the back seat of the car. *That's* how strong the feeling was.

It ended up following me home too. It wasn't until later that night that I realized what it was. And my whole understanding of death and the *after* changed.

As per my usual routine, I took a shower and grabbed something to eat before heading up to bed, since I was at work early the next day too.

It was around midnight when I finally started getting dozy. I was just about to be lulled to sleep when something made me jolt upright; the sound of a door creaking. I had a habit of leaving my bedroom door partially ajar, because I didn't like the feeling of enclosed spaces, but when I glanced up, the door was fully open. I knew I hadn't left it like that, and seeing the darkness pooling through the doorframe definitely creeped me out.

I managed to rationalize my thoughts, and told myself I must have left a window open somewhere, and the draught had made the door swing open like that.

Despite the anxieties now gnawing at me, I got up to close the door again, then tried to fall back asleep. But I couldn't. The feeling of someone being inside the room with me was growing, and it got to the point where I couldn't ignore it.

I liked to think I was a pretty brave person, especially given how I have to deal with death every single day, and this was the first time I felt genuinely scared of something I couldn't actually *see*. My mind started working overdrive, wondering if maybe someone had managed to sneak inside my house while I was at work, but I knew it wasn't that. This was the same feeling that had followed me all the way from the morgue; it wasn't a human threat, but something else.

I didn't want to admit it at the time, but it felt like something had latched onto me or something. A spirit, some kind of entity, I didn't really know. But I couldn't shake the feeling that I wasn't alone. That something was watching me from the shadows.

Somehow, I managed to force those concerns from my mind and manage to fall asleep, and I didn't wake up again until my alarm went off at seven o'clock the next morning.

As soon as I opened my eyes, they went straight to the door, which was once again sitting wide open.

I got ready for work as quick as I could, then left the house. The feelings from last night had already dissipated, so I managed to chalk it down to simply being overworked and tired.

But that wasn't the last of it. A few weeks later, something similar happened.

Another spirit followed me home. That's the only explanation I can think of for the things I saw and experienced.

As someone who deals with the recently deceased, I suppose I'm the prime candidate for a haunting. I just never expected it to happen, especially not after working there for so long without any previous incidents.

It was another late shift, though I wasn't at the morgue alone this time. I had one of my co-workers with me, since we'd just received a couple of bodies from a bad car accident. It was some time after eight when I started to get a horrible throbbing pain behind my eyes. I tried to push through, but it only got worse as the evening went on, and I knew there was a possibility of it turning into a migraine, so ended up leaving a bit earlier than when my usual shift finished.

I was heading back to the office to collect my things when I heard the soft pad of footsteps walking behind me. Assuming it was my coworker, I turned to speak with him, only the corridor behind me was empty. There was nobody there.

Assuming it was simply the displacement of sound from somewhere else in the building, I continued walking, but now I couldn't shake off the feeling that there was someone behind me.

I hurriedly grabbed my belongings and left without saying goodbye to my colleague, since I was pretty eager to get out of there at this point.

My headache was still going strong, but I made it home in one piece.

I kept most of my medication in the bathroom cabinet, so I went rummaging around for some strong paracetamol that I could take to combat the intense pain in my head.

Once I'd found what I was looking for, I closed the cabinet, and froze.

For just a second, I thought I'd seen something in the mirror on the back of the cabinet. It was what I could only describe as a shadow hanging over me, or standing directly behind me. No features, but definitely humanoid. Startled, I turned around, but there was nothing there.

It freaked me out, but I assumed that maybe it was just my throbbing head messing with me.

I took some tablets and put a cold compress on my head before laying down on my bed. Gradually the throbbing started to ease, but I couldn't shake away the image of that shadowy figure standing behind me in the mirror. Was that what was causing this horrible migraine? Had something followed me back from the hospital again?

I never did get any real answers, but I've had several more experiences since then, and I'm fairly certain now that each time, it's some kind of spirit or entity that had followed me back from the morgue. They never stick around, so maybe it's simply some kind of lingering energy that somehow manages to attach to me when I'm working with the deceased. But who really knows?

CHAPTER

16

THE ASYLUM

A couple years ago me and a few friends of mine signed up to be a part of an amateur ghost hunting adventure. Basically, it was an opportunity for us to go out with some experienced people to a location to see if we could capture evidence of the paranormal. Really to me it was an opportunity to scare my girlfriend and my friend Alex, an avid skeptic when it came to anything supernatural.

This particular event was set at an old mental asylum that was located about 75 miles away from the city we lived in. It was shut down in the early part of the 1900s due to inhumane conditions in which the patients were being housed. Rumor had it a lot of people had died there over the years, and it is considered one the most haunted locations in the eastern part of the United States.

There were about six of us that were participating that day, the four of us and a couple from out of town. Eric, the guy who was supervising the experience gave each of us a map of the general layout of the place with specific locations highlighted that were supposed to be hotspots of paranormal activity. In addition to this we were each given a digital recorder to capture EVPs and a digital video camera that could detect thermal images.

We were given instructions that we had a total of six hours to complete our exploration after which he would take what we'd recorded and send us copies of anything interesting that we'd captured while there.

My friend Stacey and I paired off with each other and went to explore. We decided that hitting all of the highlighted sections was our best opportunity to experience something while we were there. Sure I was a little nervous about it but if I'd come here so I could push my limits not to play it safe.

Of all the locations I was excited to visit, none caused more apprehension than the old morgue that was located in the basement of the building. We decided that would be the last place we would visit hoping the spirits would be most active the later it got at night.

The other hotspots included the Warden's Office, the Infirmary, and The Isolation Rooms. All of these we intended on checking out at some point that evening in addition to walking around some of the wards and patient rooms to see if we could capture anything on video or the digital recorder.

The sun was starting to dip behind the horizon when we first entered the building. Despite its age a lot of the green and white tiles were still in place in the front lobby and other than dust piling up in the corners and some sun bleaching here and there I wouldn't have thought it had been nearly a hundred years since this place last was open.

The strangest thing was the building itself didn't give me that eerie feeling just standing there. I'd expected there to be an energy hanging in the air that made me feel like something was waiting for me. Instead, it just felt empty. Already I was starting to doubt the validity of claims that had been made about the asylum which if I was being honest with myself helped me to relax.

For the first couple hours Stacey and I walked around the halls and the main living areas asking questions like "Is anyone there?" and "Is there something we can do to help you move on from this place?" Despite our good intentions we didn't hear anything that would indicate that something was trying to contact us or took notice of our presence for that matter. In the end the recordings that we took during that time proved this to be true.

I'd say it was around 10:00 at night when we finally decided it was time to get serious and go through the locations where we were told there was the highest amount of activity.

The closest one happened to be the isolation rooms where they housed some of the most dangerous people while the asylum was open. On our way there we decided we would each take a turn being locked in the room for a total of 10 minutes attempting to communicate with any spirits left there.

I offered to be the first one to go inside. The room itself was a small square. No bed was visible anywhere and the walls were covered in a fabric and stuffing looked to be poking through holes almost everywhere.

The sun had already set, and the only light was a thin sliver coming from beneath the door cast by the flashlights we'd brought with us. As soon as I sat down and turned on the recorder the atmosphere in the room completely changed. Since we'd begun, I hadn't felt like there was anything with us. Now the sense of someone looming over the top of me was so overwhelming I couldn't help but look behind me even in the pitch dark.

I closed my eyes and managed a weak, "Hello?"

I swear at that moment I heard a man whisper in my ear, "Please, let me out of here."

Despite how quiet it was I could hear the pain and anguish impregnating every word. If I hadn't been so terrified at that moment, I would have felt bad for whoever was stuck in here with me. A sound like something being torn began right behind me.

It's just a mouse in the stuffing, that's all. Nothing to worry about.

I tried to hold onto the thought, but I couldn't get the image of someone raking their fingernails along the padded walls repeatedly. The feeling of hopelessly being cut off from everything I cared about washed over me so strongly I dropped the recorder and collapsed on the floor. Sobs wracked my body so strongly I couldn't even move. In my mind I was begging Stacey to open the door and let me out, but I couldn't make a noise to get her to help me. It was like I was completely paralyzed there on that floor.

Just as quickly as it had come the feeling seemed to disappear completely. It was such a shift in emotion I sat up and had to think if it had been real or just my mind reeling from such a hyper-stressed state.

I scooted over to the door and knocked letting Stacey know I wanted to be let out. When her face came into view, I could see the laughter in her grin since I hadn't lasted the full 10 minutes. The smile fell almost immediately as soon as she looked at me. It must have been apparent that something had happened in the room and I was pretty shaken by it.

As scared as I was I wanted to check something. I took the thermal camera and pointed it at the back wall of the room where I'd heard the ripping noise coming from. Although we said we wanted to experience the supernatural seeing what was on the screen had me questioning that desire.

The entire room was a cold blue except for two

places. One was the spot where I'd been laying a moment before, the other was against the wall. Five vertical lines stood out in bright yellow. It looked exactly like someone had drug their fingers along the wall.

"That was you right?" she asked me. All I could do was shake my head.

I spent the next minute telling her what I'd heard and felt while inside there. Part of me wanted her to doubt me so I could brush it off a little myself but there was no hesitation when she said, "Hell no, I'm not going in there." I wanted to make fun of her for chickening out, but in her position and knowing what I'd just experienced I wouldn't go in either. Frankly, if she would have told me she wanted to leave right then I wouldn't have argued with her.

We quickly left the isolation cells behind trying to get as much distance between ourselves and whatever was there. The next two places we visited were the Warden's office and the infirmary. Whether the spirits weren't present, or they took pity on us I don't know but we weren't able to capture anything on either device. Even the empty feeling had returned but both of us knew, me more than Stacey, that was a lie.

By my watch it was almost 12:30 pm and we still had one more room we wanted to check out. The Morgue. What happened in the isolation cell was bad enough and now it felt like we were going to someplace even darker. I didn't think though that anything could be worse than what already happened so we followed the map to the stairs leading to the basement.

The halls were made of concrete and had been painted an off white color. Some of the paint was chipped off in places but was mainly intact. There was also a definite dip in the temperature of the air down there too. Stacey must have felt it as well because I saw here rub her arms with her hands trying to get some warmth in them.

I checked the map and it said the morgue was located just up ahead through the first door on the right. I think we both were a little tense and remained quiet as we made our way to the door. Standing in front of it I noticed it was definitely wider than a normal door, probably to make space for a gurney to be wheeled through.

I looked over at Stacey trying to read her thoughts but she just kept her eyes on the door. I took this as an affirmative and turned the handle and pushed into the space beyond.

Walking in I expected to see metal tables and surgical implements left behind almost as if they were abandoned mid procedure. The reality was much less. In front of me stood an empty rectangular room. The only sign this was used for anything but storage was a track system on the ceiling where I assumed curtains were hung while this place was still in operation. I knew my metal images had been based on what I'd seen in the movies, but this was underwhelming to say the least.

To my right I notice a door that I hadn't seen when I came in, but it just led to another small square room which was also empty. This is where we decided to set up and try and communicate with any spirits that might wish to speak with us. Just to add a little extra to the experience we decided to turn off our lights and ask our questions in the complete darkness.

We started asking questions, trying to illicit any sort of response whether it be spoken or a sound but for 10 minutes nothing happened other than us talking to an empty room. Out of nowhere though Stacey said something that didn't make sense.

"You know, you grabbing my arm isn't going to scare me you know."

The thing was, I hadn't moved and I was far enough away from her that I wouldn't be able to reach anyways. Suddenly the room felt like it got 20 degrees colder.

"I'm not grabbing your arm." I told her.

"Stop it already. This isn't funny." She was trying to keep her voice light, but I could hear the fear that had crept into it. Then she screamed.

When a person screams when they're truly

scared it is a full body reaction. Every muscle tenses, you use all the air in your lungs for that one act. This is what Stacey did, repeatedly. I don't know how long it took me to break out of the shock I was in but when I did I scrambled for my flashlight but I ended up knocking away from me in panic.

On my hands and knees I crawled in the direction I thought it went, blindly probing the area in front of me. During this time Stacey continued to scream as panic took a firmer hold. Finally I find the flashlight and fumble for the button momentarily before I manage to turn it on.

I point it directly at Stacey who has gone sheet white and has fallen over in the fetal position with her arms wrapped tightly around herself. I move over towards her and place my hand on her which causes her to flinch and scream once more.

"Stacey, it's me. You're okay."

Her eyes pop open, meet mine and her body

begins to finally relax. She leaps at me and wraps her arms around my neck sobbing. From what I heard her say then and after she repeated the story later what seemed like hundreds of hands grabbed her all at once. Even though they were ice cold it felt like they were burning her skin.

As soon as she was able to get up off the floor the two of us ran the entire way out of the asylum. I didn't care how much longer we had left to explore. After what had happened to the two of us, we didn't want to spend another minute in that evil place.

When we turned in our equipment, we told Eric that we had no interest in receiving any copies of the recordings that we made that night. It was a part of our lives the two of us would rather leave back in that place where it belongs. Hopefully for good.

AVAILABLE NOW ON AMAZON

CHAPTER

1

PROLOGUE

FALL 1958

Sylvia absently dried the dishes with a cloth as she stared through the window at the gathering dusk. She was helping her mother clean up after dinner while her father lounged in the living room, watching the news on the television.

As the shadows lengthened outside, covering the lawn with darkness, she found her own reflection staring back at her, all blonde hair and green eyes and a young, slender face. She blinked, looking away. It always got so dark in the evenings now that Fall was almost over.

The mornings, too. When she had to wake up early for work, the sky was still curtained with the dregs of dusk, the moon still a bright sliver in the sky. She'd only recently started her new job as a receptionist, so she was still getting used to waking up before the sun was out.

"Sylvia?"

Realizing her mother was calling her name, she turned away from the window, snapping out of her own thoughts. "Yes, mama?" She asked, her blond ringlets falling over her shoulder.

"Tomorrow, I was thinking of doing some baking," her mother said as she dried her hands on the apron around her waist.

Sylvia's eyes glistened, nodding enthusiastically. "Please let me help you. You know I love baking in the Fall. We can make pumpkin bread and apple pie and scones and-"

"Margret," her father shouted from the other room, interrupted her excited ramble. "Come look at this."

Exchanging a glance with her daughter, Margret set down the bowl she was about to put away in the cupboard and went into the living room, Sylvia at her heels.

Her father was still sitting in his armchair, watching the television. The news was playing, the volume turned up high.

"Tragedy has struck at Frost Falls," the news reporter said, making Sylvia's eyes widen. Tragedy? What kind of tragedy? She rested her hands against the back of her father's worn leather armchair, watching over his shoulder.

"Yesterday evening, a fire broke out at Frost Fall's luxurious lodge. This morning, after emergency services took to the scene, the incident still remains a mystery. How did the fire break out and cause so many casualties without warning? Who was responsible for the blaze? Was it an act of arson, or an unfortunate accident? We're still waiting to hear updates from the local fire department, and many residents are waiting for answers to the tragic event."

Sylvia put a hand to her mouth as the reporter continued.

"We have been informed that there have been two confirmed deaths from the fire, as well as a number of casualties. But three of the lodge's guests have been reported as missing. We hope to have more information soon."

The report turned to a weather forecast, and Sylvia's father turned the volume down again as Margret sank onto the sofa in shock.

"A fire at the lodge. How could that have happened?" She said, shaking her head.

Sylvia stayed quiet, heartbroken for the lives that were lost, and those that were injured.

She found herself remembering the last time she'd walked past the lodge; one beautiful morning a few weeks ago. She'd had a book tucked under her arm as she walked past the hotel in search of somewhere to read. Fall had always been her favorite season, watching the leaves turn shades of red and orange and yellow, falling from the trees and dancing on the wind. On weekends, her favorite thing to do was find a bench overlooking the river and read her novels, transport herself into different stories, different lives.

This particular weekend, though, had been different. As she walking past the lodge, her gaze drawn to the sun glinting off the chimney, she'd walked straight into someone she hadn't seen coming towards her. Her book had gone flying out of her hands, a soft gasp of surprise parting her lips as she stared at the man in front of her. She remembered him being incredibly handsome, a little bit older than her, perhaps somewhere in his early- to mid-twenties. And his smile… a smile she hadn't been able to forget since. He had apologized profusely, reaching down to retrieve her book for her. And when he handed it back and their eyes met, it was like something inside her had awoken.

She still remembered every word of their exchange.

"I-I'm so sorry, I wasn't watching where I was going," Sylvia had said, tucking a blond ringlet behind her ear as she sheepishly looked down at her feet.

The man had chuckled, shaking his head. "I'm just as to blame," he said, giving her another charming smile. Then he'd looked up at the lodge, his eyes glowing amber in the sun. "It's a beautiful building, isn't it?"

Sylvia had nodded, clutching her book tightly to her chest. "The most beautiful building in town," she'd told him. "Are you new here?" She'd cocked her head curiously.

"I'm staying here for a few months," he'd told her, gesturing up to the lodge. "The moment I saw this place, I felt it calling to me."

Sylvia found herself completely entranced with his voice, his smile, everything about his countenance, and she'd been unable to help herself from asking. "What... What's your name, if I may ask?"

And the man had smiled, and given her a charming flourish as he introduced himself. "Henry," he'd told her. "My name is Henry."

The memory faded, and Sylvia found herself back to the present, Henry's name on her lips as hoped that he hadn't been one of the unfortunate victims of the lodge fire.

CHAPTER

1

Madison gripped the wheel tighter as the car bounced and trundled over the rutted path, twigs and gravel crunching together beneath the tires. With each jolt, more strands of dark hair fell over her hazel eyes, and she impatiently brushed them aside, squinting at the road in concentration.

"Are we almost there?" Eva asked from the passenger seat, resting her elbows against her knees as she gazed through the window, watching the dark trees pass by. In contrast to Madison's loose curls, Eva's blond hair was scraped up into a ponytail, tied with one of her favorite pink scrunchies. She turned her head excitedly as a break in the trees gave her a glimpse of the snowy mountain ranges beyond, their peaks almost breaking through the clouds. Then the forest took over again, shadows falling across the window.

"Almost," Madison said, squinting against the dappled sunlight falling through the canopy overhead, creating crisscrossing patterns along the windshield. "At least, I think we are. I haven't seen a signpost in a bit."

Eva glanced across at her, an amused curl to her lip. "You haven't gotten us lost, have you?"

"No," Madison said defensively. "It's this way, I'm sure." She flicked a glance at the GPS, which hadn't updated their position in a while. Either the signal was terrible out here, or the route hadn't been updated in a while. Either way, she was certain she was heading towards Frost Falls.

Eva chuckled, leaning back against the headrest. "I've been looking forward to this for ages. It's been too long since we took a trip together like this."

Madison nodded distractedly. "I know. I'll be glad when we get there though." *Glad for the rest*, she added in her head. The truth was, she'd only really agreed to accompany Eva on this trip out of her own sense of guilt. She knew it had been far too long since they'd done anything like this together; their jobs occupied most of their time, and whenever they did try and arrange something, their schedules always clashed. When Eva had brought up the town of Frost Falls and the grand reopening of it's lodge, she thought it would be a good opportunity to spend some more time with her friend. But then she'd learned about its strange history, and her expectations had been dashed. While Eva was a firm believer of the paranormal, Madison couldn't say the same about herself.

"I can't believe the lodge opened again after all this time," Eva observed as she watched the forest pass by, glimpsing snowy mountains in the distance. "Hasn't it literally been like seventy years since the place was closed down?"

"Yeah. Why did it shut down again?"

"There was a fire or something," Eva said, tapping her fingers against her chin. "I couldn't find too many details about it. But the place just fell off the map. I was surprised when they announced the reopening so suddenly."

"I'm just excited to get a break from everything," Madison said, shaking her head.

The car broke away from the trees, and a stream of sunlight fell across the windshield, highlighting the streaks of dirt in the corners. "Work's been getting so hectic lately. I just need some time to rewind and give myself a rest, you know?"

Eva laughed, nodding. "Tell me about it." Her expression turned serious again a second later, and she leaned back with a soft sigh. As much as she loved working as a vet assistant, the job certainly had its own challenges. Being an animal lover was both a blessing and a curse, especially when things didn't always go the way they hoped.

Noticing her friend's crestfallen expression, Madison threw her a glance, shifting her hands on the wheel. "Everything okay?"

Eva quickly forced herself to perk up, but Madison had known her long enough to see straight through her feigned cheerfulness. "Sorry. I was just thinking about Milo."

Madison was quiet for a second before speaking. "Is that the dog you had to…"

"Put down, yeah," Eva said, gazing solemnly through the window. "I know I shouldn't get attached, but I just… he was so sweet, you know? He was in our care for almost two months and I just fell in love with his little face." She swallowed back the emotion bubbling at the back of her throat at the thought of the GoldenDoodle. He'd suddenly developed a malignant form of cancer that his owner hadn't been able to afford to treat. Only a week before she was due to go on this vacation, she'd had to assist the vet in putting him down. It had completely broke her.

"I'm sorry," Madison said softly, reaching out to squeeze her friend's arm.

"Thank you," Eva said, taking in a shaky breath. "I know it was for the best. He's free of pain now."

The two of them fell into a comfortable silence, watching the fields of frosted yellow flowers pass by as the car trundled along, until Eva eventually twisted round in her seat, facing Madison with a half-mischievous grin, recovering her good mood. "So… do you think the rumors about Frost Falls are true?" She quirked her brow as Madison furrowed hers.

"What, you mean the ghost stories?" She said dubiously. "You know I don't believe in that kind of thing." And she didn't. She hated anything remotely creepy or to do with ghosts. She refused to watch scary movies, no matter how many times Eva asked, and Halloween was her least favorite holiday. If anything, the whole Halloween thing freaked her out. When she was younger, she'd had a neighbor called Mr. Dubois, who was a rather strange character. All throughout her childhood, he had decorated his lawn every year with Halloween decorations and kids always flocked to his house for sweets. But he'd always struck Madison as being sad. Then, one Halloween night, he'd taken his own life. Instead of enjoying a fun night of trick or treating, Madison had stayed inside while the street was flooded with emergency vehicles and chaos. It was something she'd never been able to forget, and getting into the spirit of all things spooky had never seemed right since then.

Eva pouted. "You're so boring."

"*But* I do find old places fascinating," she said in an attempt to appease her friend's disappointment. "Whether the stories are true or not, I think it'll be a fun place to explore and learn more about."

The fields gave way to another thick copse of trees, and the winter sunlight disappeared behind the thick canopy, plunging the inside of the car into a sudden gloom. Eva shivered slightly as the air turned chilled.

"Apparently the fire was a huge tragedy," Eva continued, frowning in thought as she recounted what she'd read online before setting off for the trip. "That's why the lodge closed down and the town became reclusive. Bad press, I guess. Nobody went there anymore."

"That's just what the stories online tell you," Madison pointed out. "I'm sure it's not as bad as it sounds. People like gossip, that's all." As a journalist for a local newspaper, Madison knew all about tabloid gossip and fake news. Some of the stories she'd had to research in the past had led to dead end after dead end as she searched for the root of the story. Sometimes, the more talked about something was, the less reliable the story.

Eva hummed to herself. "People who've visited have had strange experiences though," she said, the shadows of the forest casting her face into gloom. "There's a full forum online where people share their stories."

Madison gave her a sideway glance. "And how many of them are made up for attention?"

Eva shrugged. "They seemed legit to me."

"Hm," Madison muttered, gripping the wheel tighter as she switched on her high beams to cut through the forest's silhouette. "We should be nearly there."

"You said that half-an-hour ago," Eva mused, enjoying the irk in Madison's expression. "But I'm sure you're right. It's definitely getting chillier up here."

Aptly named, Frost Falls was a small town buried between two snowy mountains. As out of the way it was, Madison wasn't surprised it had fallen off the map after briefly gaining fame as a tourist attraction back in the early 1930s. She only knew what little research Eva had done before coming, but after hearing about the lodge's grand reopening, and the town's unusual history, it had seemed the perfect time to take a break from work and indulge her own curiosity.

The edge of the forest was almost in sight when something small and black plummeted down from the treetops, hitting the car's hood with a sickening thud.

Eva screamed as Madison slammed her foot down on the break, sending the car to a screeching halt, twigs and bracken hitting the window.

"W-what the hell was that?" Eva gasped, her eyes wide as she gazed through the front window.

Madison ignored her, her heart thudding dully in her chest as she stared at the small black figure lying unmoving on the hood. It looked like a crow or a raven, its feathers the color of ink. Its eyes were wide open, staring at them with an unnatural stare. A streak of dark blood seeped across the hood's paintwork from the bird's broken body.

"Oh my god," Eva said as Madison unclipped her seatbelt and opened her car door, letting in a stream of cold air. "Where did it come from?"

"I don't know," Madison said as she stepped out. The wind beneath the trees had an icy touch, and she subconsciously wrapped her arms around herself. "It came from above, I think." She glanced up, at the thick, intertwining canopy of dark foliage, but she could see nothing up there.

"Is it dead?" Eva asked, climbing out of her side.

Madison swallowed uneasily at the sight of the blood, the bird's crooked neck, its open eyes. "Yeah, I think so."

"Poor thing," Eva murmured. "What do we do?"

Madison shook her head. "We need to move it, I guess. We can't exactly keep driving with it just lying there."

"Right."

Madison bit her lip, debating how to get it off the car without touching it with her hands. Birds were known to carry diseases, and given the way it had simply fallen out of the sky, there was a chance it had been killed by some kind of sickness.

"How about this?" Eva said, bringing a plastic shopping bag from the trunk of the car.

Madison nodded. "That'll do. Thanks." Folding the bag several times to create a thicker barrier, she used it like a glove to pick the bird's body up and set it down on the soil by the side of the road.

"That's so sad," Eva muttered, eyeing the bird. "I hope it died quickly."

"Come on, let's get going," Madison said, scrunching the bag up and putting it back in the trunk to dispose of later. "There's nothing more we can do for it."

"Do you think that was a sign or something?" Eva said as she climbed back into the car.

Madison gave her a narrow look. "Are you trying to tell me we're cursed now or something?"

Eva shrugged. "Maybe it's some kind of omen."

Madison scoffed. "You read too many of those forum stories," she said, trying not to stare at the blood on the hood, a single black feather fluttering in the wind. She'd have to find a car wash once they got to town. "I'm sure it's nothing. Just a cruel act of nature. That's all."

CHAPTER

2

"There it is!" Eva said excitedly as Madison pulled the car up to a small parking lot outside of a large, wooden log cabin, and killed the engine. She fumbled excitedly with her seatbelt, all of the sadness and regret about her job fading away the moment she stared up at the building.

"We finally made it," Madison said, stretching her arms over her head with a yawn. "It was a longer drive than I expected."

Despite Madison's fatigue from travelling, Eva had completely regained her energy, and was almost vibrating with excitement as she peered out at the cabin, gleaming as it was beneath the wintery sun. The two of them had always been complete opposites; Madison calm and mellow, Eva loud and excitable. But their friendship had bloomed all the way back in eighth grade, and almost ten years later, they were still just as close as they had been then. Eva was the one who had suggested taking the trip to Frost Falls after reading about its reopening, and the strange mysteries and rumors that seemed to surround the town, tucked away in the middle of nowhere. Madison had always been fascinated by history, and Eva was naturally drawn to stories of the paranormal, so it seemed a perfect fit for the two of them to spend some much-needed time together.

Eva climbed out first, a wide grin spreading along her face as she gazed up at the lodge. Madison remained in the car for another few seconds, trying to push away her tiredness and recover some of her own excitement about the trip. She forced a smile onto her face and stepped out after her.

"Come on, let's go check in, then take a look around," Eva said. "We can bring our bags in later."

Madison nodded and locked the car behind her before following her friend up to the lodge's main reception, trying not to look at the blood on the hood as she passed.

After checking in with the lodge's friendly staff, Eva and Madison took a brief tour of the building.

Branching off from the main lobby and reception area was a communal space, with wooden beams crisscrossing the ceiling and a fire crackling away in the hearth. The walls were timber, studded with rustic charm in the form of paintings and wool blankets that were draped across the room to create a cozy atmosphere. There were different sizes of couches and seating areas spread around the room, and a wide coffee table in the center with some books and magazines splayed across it. A large television screen hung above the fire, and bookshelves full of puzzles and more books were sat either side of the mantel. Despite the warmth radiating from the fire and the cozy ambience of the room, Madison felt a strange chill on her neck that she couldn't seem to shake, as though all the décor was just a front for something else. She figured it might be because of the more modern renovations after the fire, but something about it all seemed to artificial.

If Eva had the same thought, she didn't show it, gazing around the open lounge with a grin on her face. "It's so lovely," she said. "And look, they even have a dining room through there."

Madison followed her gaze, to a pair of wooden double doors on the other side of the communal area. The windows were frosted, but she glimpsed the outline of tables and chairs on the other side. "That must be where we can get breakfast," she said. "Although we didn't pay extra for it, I don't think."

Eva shrugged. "We can pay later if we feel like it. Let's go and check out our room!"

Madison nodded, her gaze lingering on the burning fire for a second longer before following her friend upstairs.

If there were any other guests staying there, they were nowhere to be seen, and the strange emptiness made Madison feel uneasy about the place, but she forced herself to brush it off.

"What room are we in?" Eva asked as they headed upstairs to the guest rooms.

Madison glanced down at the old, rusty key in her hand, and the small label attached to it. "Room 6, on the second floor."

"Great."

They climbed the stairs up to the second floor, the wooden boards creaking underfoot and the fire a distant crackle, and paused at the end of the corridor.

Madison slotted the key in the lock and pushed open the door. It shuddered slightly, as though there was some kind of resistance on the other side, before swinging open, revealing a warm, well-furnished room.

"Wow," Eva breathed, hurrying inside before Madison. "It's gorgeous."

The furnishings were all wooden, with red and gold accents, giving the room an almost elegant, luxurious feel. There was a log dresser and wardrobe on one side of the room, with two beds pressed up against opposite walls, a wide curtained window between them, overlooking the forest that bordered the lodge. A door beside the dresser led to a small, ensuite bathroom.

Madison looked around, relaxing into a more genuine smile. It was a beautiful place, both inside and out, and she could definitely see herself getting a much-needed break here. She was looking forward to exploring the town later too, and seeing what kind of history it offered. As a writer, she was naturally inclined towards expanding her knowledge, including learning more about the histories of places and people previously unfamiliar to her. In all honesty, if she hadn't been so intrigued by learning more about Frost Falls, she probably wouldn't have come on this trip at all. She'd had to force herself not to listen to Eva's ghost stories about the place and focus on the rustic charm of the village that was what enticed her here in the first place.

Eva collapsed onto one of the beds with a relaxed sigh. "This is so nice," she said.

Madison's gaze was drawn to the other side of the room to the bathroom, where an old hearth had been blocked off with dark wooden beams. She wondered briefly why it was out of use, but figured it could have been a safety measure, to prevent guests from being reckless with fire. After all, hadn't the lodge been closed due to some kind of fire in the past?

"Let's go and bring out bags up," Eva suggested. "As soon as we finish unpacking, we can head into town and grab some lunch."

Madison nodded. "Sure."

They headed back downstairs, passing through the empty communal room. The fire had died down a little since they were last there, and the shadows around the room had deepened, making Madison look away uneasily. Maybe it was Eva's talk of ghosts and mysteries that had set her on edge, but she couldn't seem to shake off the feeling that something was *off* about the place. She just didn't know what.

Hurrying after Eva, they passed back through the reception room, with its more modern furnishings and large wooden desk, and retrieved their luggage from the trunk of the car. Madison had managed to pack everything into one suitcase and a small carry-all, while Eva had brought several cases of varying sizes.

When Madison raised her brow, her friend shrugged. "I didn't know what kind of clothes to pack," she said, hauling her luggage behind her. "I need to be prepared for all kinds of weather."

Madison shook her head. "Clues in the name," she said. "The only weather we'll be seeing up here is snow and ice."

Eva ignored her, marching ahead with her suitcase wheels snagging in the thin layer of snow on the ground.

Madison made sure they hadn't left anything behind, then followed after her. As she walked back towards the lodge, something moved in her periphery, and her gaze was drawn up to the front-facing windows of the lodge. Judging from the view out of their window, their room was the second one along from the left. Squinting against the winter sun, she thought she saw someone standing at their window, peering down at them with a pale face. But then it was gone, and Madison was left blinking, wondering if it had been there at all.

After unpacking everything into their room, Madison and Eva decided to head into town. Madison was still a little shaken by what she'd seen in the window, but after checking their room and finding nobody there, she assumed it must have been nothing but a trick of the light, or her own tired brain conjuring things that weren't there.

It was just after two o'clock in the afternoon when they made it into town, and the morning sun had been replaced by a heavy overcast sky. There was a bitter chill in the air that made Madison glad she'd worn her thermals, though her cheeks were already starting to go red and numb.

Parking the car near the Frost Fall's visitor's center, the two of them headed inside for a map and some guidance about where to start their exploration.

A young woman was sitting at the reception desk, a stand of leaflets sitting on the side. Her startlingly red hair was tied neatly in a bun, contrasting to the chalky pallor of her skin beneath the glaring fluorescents.

She glanced up when they walked in, smiling. "Good afternoon," she said, tucking a strand of crimson hair behind her ear.

Madison returned her smile while Eva did the talking. "Hiya. We've just arrived at Frost Falls, and we were wondering if you could help us with any local history tours."

The woman nodded, standing up. "Of course. You've come to the right place," she said. "We offer one-on-one tours of Frost Falls, as well as group ones. Although the last tour group just left, so…"

"It's okay. We'll take a one-on-one," Eva said before she could consult with Madison. "That's alright, isn't it?"

Madison nodded. She would rather it just be the two of them, rather than being stuck with a group of strangers anyway.

"Great. Give me a second, and I'll go ahead and arrange that for you."

"Thanks."

While the woman disappeared into the back office, Madison browsed some of the leaflets on display. "They have a museum here too," she said as her eye caught the information booklet for Frost Falls Museum. "Might be worth checking out."

"Of course," Eva said. "We're not leaving until we've explored every inch of this place… and seen a ghost!"

Madison pursed her lips at Eva's words, but said nothing.

"Right," the woman said as she came back to the front desk, "I can book a tour with a guide called Alex. Is there a particular time you'd like to meet?"

Eva glanced at Madison, who pursed her lips in thought. "Maybe half three?" She suggested. "We can grab lunch first, then meet up for the tour."

"Sounds good to me," Eva agreed, turning back to the woman. "Half-three, if that's possible."

"Of course. I'll book that right now. Here's a map of the meeting place, and Alex's number in case you need to get in touch. If you have any other questions or queries, we're open until ten o'clock tonight."

"Thank you very much," Madison said, tucking the details away in her pocket as Eva clasped her hands excitedly.

"Have a lovely day."

"I'm stuffed," Eva said, patting her stomach dramatically as they left the small Italian restaurant and stepped out onto the street. "That was some of the best pizza I've ever had."

Madison chuckled at her friend's exaggeration. "It was good, but I wouldn't say it's the best I've ever had," she said honestly. "Still, a very nice couple who run the place. We should go there again before the trip's over."

Eva nodded enthusiastically. "I agree," she said with a laugh. "Anyway, what time is it? When did we say we were meeting our tour guide?"

Madison checked her watch. "It's quarter-past-three. We said we'd meet at half-past, outside the museum."

"And where exactly is the museum?" Eva asked, gazing at the street around her. The town was more rustic than she'd been expecting, with old-fashioned storefronts and chipped cobblestones running alongside the more modernized tarmac road.

Madison rolled her eyes, but kept smiling. "Near the visitor's center. So back the way we came."

"Oh, easy enough," Eva said cheerfully, patting Madison's arm. "Let's go and see who our guide is."

They reached the museum a few minutes before half-past, scanning the crowd for anyone who might resemble a tour guide. There was a cluster of tourists standing by the front doors, but standing off to the side, leaning against the low brick wall, was a young man.

"Alex?" Eva said tentatively as they approached him, eyeing the lanyard around his neck that read *PRIVATE TOURS*.

The man looked up, smiling. He was tall, with a mop of dark hair and dark eyes, and looked to be close to their age, somewhere in his early- to mid- twenties. "That's me."

Eva grinned, offering her hand. "I'm Eva. This is my friend, Madison."

Madison nodded in return, keeping her hands tucked in her pockets. "Hello," she said politely.

"I'm Alex, as I'm sure you already know. It's a pleasure to meet you both," he said, then swept his arms in a wide motion. "So, Frost Falls… where would you like to start?"

Eva and Madison exchanged a glance. "Museum?" They both said, then smiled.

Alex chuckled. "Of course," he said, "a staple of Frost Falls' history. Why don't you follow me."

He skirted past the group of tourists, who were being led by another guide, and ushered the two of them inside the small building. The whole museum was tucked into one open space, with portioned walls and arrows pointing from one exhibit to another in an orderly fashion. Alex took them to the first glass case, which held a series of old documents and maps showing the foundation of the town in the local area. Madison gazed over them all with a curious gaze, reading everything on the information stands beside the exhibits and storing the knowledge away in her mind. As a writer, she never knew when such information might come in useful.

"The town of Frost Falls was established sometime in the early 1800s," Alex explained as he gestured to the documents, "so it has quite a history."

"Lots of ghost stories?" Eva quipped, a mischievous sparkle in her eyes.

Alex's brows rose up. "Are you interested in the paranormal?" He asked.

Eva nodded eagerly. "Ever since I saw a ghost when I was younger, I've been *fascinated* by the possibility of life after death," she explained, getting the usual glimmer in her eye when she talked about her passion. "I'm always curious to know if other people have had similar experiences, especially places like this…"

While the two of them chatted, Madison let her gaze drift around the small museum, taking pictures on her phone. She'd left her camera back at their room at the lodge, not sure if she'd be using it, but now she regretted it as they toured around the old building. There was already so much history packed into such a small space.

Madison drifted behind them as Eva and Alex paused in front of the exhibit for the late 1900s era of Frost Falls. There was a number of old, black-and-white photographs preserved behind the case. A couple of them had the appearance of being charred around the edges, the paper curled and blackened.

"What about the fire?" Madison heard Eva ask, tucking a strand of hair sheepishly behind her ear.

"Ah yes, the infamous fire of '58," Alex recounted in a dramatic voice, flashing Eva a charming grin that made her cheeks blush involuntarily. "A very strange and mysterious story."

Madison's curiosity peaked, and she pulled away from one of the exhibit's to listen to Alex's speech.

"What happened?" Eva asked, her eyes already going wide.

Alex's smile faded a little. "The truth is, nobody really knows," he said, spreading his hands. "One night in 1958, the town's lodge was supposedly caught up in flames. One of the guests who were staying there was said to accidentally catch his floor on fire. The blaze spread quickly through the wooden building, and people began to jump from their windows in an attempt to escape the fire. But not everyone survived the fall." Madison felt a chill touch her neck. "All the screaming and panic obviously caused locals to wake up and take a look outside. What they saw were people jumping from windows, but no flames. There was no fire."

Eva's cheeks paled, and Madison felt her throat go dry.

"What do you mean there was no fire?" Eva asked.

Alex pulled his cheeks in. "The lodge workers and some of the locals went inside to investigate. And while they found no fire, they did find black stains of smoke and ash inside some of the rooms. Nothing was burned, but there were traces of a fire having been there. Nobody knows how it happened. People call it the *Phantom Fire* of 1958."

"That can't be real," Madison muttered.

Alex chuckled. "You can still see smoke stains in parts of the lodge today," he said. "That's all the proof you need. But none of the bystanders ever saw any evidence of fire. Only the guests inside the room."

"What happened to them? Do they know who could have started the fire?" Eva asked, completely invested in the story.

Alex nodded. "All of the guests were accounted for – including those who had lost their lives jumping from the 'supposedly' burning building – apart from one family. Their bodies were never found. Some believe that one of them had started the fire and died in the flames, but that's even if there was a fire. Either way, they simply disappeared that night." He spread his hands again and shrugged. "It's all just a spooky mystery, really."

Eva glanced at Madison, grinning. "See! I told you there was something paranormal here," she said, but Madison only rolled her eyes.

"I'm sure there's a perfectly plausible explanation for what happened," she muttered, shrugging. "Or it's just a story made up for tourism."

"I don't think so," Alex interjected. "I may be a little biased, but the lodge did close down following the fire. I doubt that brought any money in."

Madison couldn't find any fault with his argument, and eventually nodded. "I guess you're right. But I'm still not buying that it's something paranormal," she added, jabbing a finger at Eva.

Eva waved her away. "I'll prove it to you, one way or another," she said cryptically, before bursting into a grin. "She's always been a sceptic," she told Alex. "She won't believe me when I say the town's haunted."

Alex flicked a glance towards Madison. "I've lived here my whole life," he said, "and I can't say I've had any particular experiences of my own. But I have heard stories, passed down from my grandparents. I try to keep an open mind, and learn a little more about the place every day."

Madison smiled faintly. "I can understand that," she said.

"Well, that concludes the tour of the museum," Alex said as they headed towards the exit. "That sums up the history of the town, pretty much. I hope you found it interesting."

"Very," the two women agreed.

After leaving the museum, Alex took them around the rest of town, pointing out buildings and objects of interest to the history of Frost Falls, which both Eva and Madison listened to with rapt attention.

"This building here is the town hall," Alex said, gesturing up to the grand building in the center of the plaza. Crumbling stone steps led up to an ornate wooden door, the dark bricks endowed with the glow of the mid-afternoon sun. "It's not used very much these days, but it's still a pretty impressive site. Currently closed to the public due to the weather, I'm afraid."

"It's a beautiful building," Madison observed, nodding.

Eva agreed, gazing up at it with a curious expression. Madison wouldn't be surprised if she was imagining the kinds of stories that might be attached to such a place.

"There's one final place I want to show you," Alex said once they'd done a circuit of the town hall's outer perimeter. "Probably my favorite."

Madison arched her brows questioningly. "What is it?"

Alex only smiled, gesturing for the two of them to follow him.

He took them deeper into town, walking past an old graveyard and a tall grey chapel with a jagged spire that almost seemed to stab the clouds above, before finally stopping outside a terracotta-colored building.

"And *this* is the gallery," Alex said with a wide grin as he led them inside to the front lobby. It was much more modern in appearance on the inside, with shiny white floors and a beautifully-pattered ceiling. "One of my favorite places in town. They host an exhibition of local artists every Spring here. It's great fun. I actually have-"

"Is that the lodge?" Madison asked, interrupting him as she walked over to one of the paintings hanging on the wall ahead of them.

Alex cleared his throat, nodding as he joined her. "Yep. Painted by a local artist back in 1924," he said. "He documented several points of interest here in Frost Falls, which you can see over here."

"That's the Town Hall," Eva said, pointing to the artwork next to it. "They're beautiful paintings. A big part of the town's history, I suppose?"

Alex nodded, his eyes glistening beneath the museum's fluorescents.

"Ah, Alex, good to see you," a female voice said from behind the three of them. A woman in formal attire stood by the lobby doors, holding a sheaf of papers.

"Hi Eliza," the tour guide said, mirroring her smile. "It's nice to see you again too."

"Are you on a tour?" The woman – Eliza – asked as she swept her gaze over Madison and Eva, a curious tilt to her lips.

Alex nodded. "Yep. Just showing them the Richardson paintings."

"Ah, lovely pieces of work, aren't they? My favorite is the one of the lodge. The way he managed to capture the serene isolation of the background, and at the same time the inviting warmth of the building itself. It used to be such a beautiful structure… before the fire, of course."

"You're familiar with the fire?" Eva asked.

Eliza chuckled, waving her papers around. "Of course. Who *isn't* familiar with the fire around here?" She pointed out, flicking a glance towards Alex. "It's a big talking point for the tourists. All the rumors and whatnot, whatever you choose to believe."

Eva opened her mouth to say something, but Eliza was already bustling away. "Anyway, I have some things to arrange. Enjoy the rest of your tour."

She swept away with a click of heels, and Alex returned his attention back to Madison and Eva, resuming his friendly grin. "Right then, if you'll follow me, I'll show you the rest of the gallery."

After paying Alex for his time, the two of them decided to walk around town on their own.

Eva looked regretful as she stared after Alex's retreating form, unable to take her eyes off him until he had disappeared completely behind the throng of people.

Madison raised her brows at her friend. "What was that about?"

Eva stared at her, feigning cluelessness. "What was what about?"

"That look you two just gave each other," Madison said. "Don't think I didn't see it. Neither of you wanted to leave each other."

Eva looked away, pressing her lips together as her cheeks turned pink. Madison had a feeling it wasn't anything to do with the cold wind this time. "I mean, he was pretty cute, don't you think?" She said with a sheepish grin. Madison laughed, already forgetting the uneasy feeling she'd had since arriving at the lodge.

"I guess. You two did look pretty nice together," she commented, making Eva grin.

"Hopefully that isn't the last we see of him," Eva said.

Madison shrugged. "You have his number, right? I'm sure he wouldn't mind hearing from you again."

Eva's grin widened as she hooked her arm through Madison's. "Alright, alright. Let's go and see what else Frost Falls has to offer."

"Look at this," Eva said, pointing to a small building tucked away at the bottom of the street, "a bookshop. Let's take a look inside."

Madison was still trying to take a photo of the old buildings that lined the street when Eva tugged restlessly on her arm, so she sighed and gave up, following her into the small, dusty bookstore.

A bell tingled softly overhead as they stepped over the threshold, and Madison's throat immediately closed up from the presence of dust. Shelves of books ran all directions, from floor to ceiling, with extra books stacked on the floor in haphazard piles.

"Afternoon."

The two of them glanced up in surprise, neither of them noticing the man standing at the counter on their left.

Eva recovered first, offering him a wide smile. "Hello!" She said.

The man must have been no younger than seventy, with a balding head and a heavily-lined face. His eyes were small and dark, reminding Madison of a raven. His smile didn't quite reach them.

Feeling a shiver of unease, Madison reached for Eva's arm and whispered under her breath that she wanted to leave. But her friend waved her off.

"I won't be long. I just want to look at the books," she said, shrugging Madison off with her usual smile. "I thought you loved places like this."

Madison said nothing, feeling the man's strange gaze on the back of her neck.

Eager to get away from it, she moved deeper into the shelves, running her gaze along the books.

From the front of the shop, she heard Eva strike up a conversation with the man.

"Were you alive when the fire happened?" She asked, making Madison wince. She really had no filter. But the man didn't seem to take her comment in a bad way.

"Yes," he said. "I was just a young man back then."

"Really?!" Eva said excitedly. "Do you think the place is haunted?"

To Madison's surprise, the man agreed. "Very much so," he said. "I'm sure you've heard the stories. The lodge is haunted by the people who died that night. *And* the man who started the fire."

"You know who it was?"

"It's been so long, I've forgotten the name," he said. "But I recall he was one of the guests staying there."

"That's crazy!"

Madison shook her head, tuning back out of the conversation. Eva was far too gullible about these things. The man was probably part of the ruse to drum up tourism in the small town.

She was about to go back to Eva when something caught her eye; a small black book sitting on the shelf. As innocuous as it first appeared, something about it piqued her interest, and she found herself reaching for it. The book had no title, no words lettered on the spine. It was made of a smooth black leather, and had an almost ageless appearance, neither new nor old.

She picked it up and flipped open the front page, her brows furrowing.

It was empty.

The searched through the whole thing, but there were no words written on any of the pages. Perhaps it was not a book at all, but a journal.

Excited about her find, she carried the black book to the front of the shop, where the old man was still fueling Eva's imagination with stories of ghosts.

When he saw what Madison was holding, he stopped short, his eyes going wide. "Where did you find that?" He asked, his voice a strangled whisper.

Madison blinked in surprise, gesturing behind her. "Just on one of the shelves."

He shook his head. "No, it shouldn't be here. It's not mine."

Madison frowned. "Oh," she said. "Maybe you just didn't realize you put it out."

The man's gaze never left the book, his cheeks looking sallow beneath the sickly fluorescents. "No, no it's not mine."

Eva glanced towards her, her eyes wide. "Ooh, a mystery," she muttered.

"I'm sorry, but I'll have to ask you to leave," the man said, his tone suddenly becoming ominous. "Please take the book with you."

Madison stared at him, unsettled by the sudden change in his demeanor. "Um, okay, how much is it?"

He shook his head, making a shooing motion. "It doesn't belong to me. I don't want any money for it. Just take it away."

With a frown, Madison dug a ten-dollar bill from her pocket and set it down on the counter, before leaving without another word.

Please remember to leave a review after reading.

AVAILABLE ON ALL PODCAST NETWORKS
CHECK OUT
— PODCASTS —
HOSTED BY EVE:

TRUE WHISPERS
A TRUE CRIME PODCAST

A TRULY HAUNTED PODCAST
A PARANORMAL PODCAST

FOREVER HAUNTED
A PARANORMAL PODCAST

BONE CHILLING TALES
A PARANORMAL PODCAST

THE GHOST THAT HAUNTS ME
A PARANORMAL PODCAST

FIND EVE
— ON —
YOUTUBE:

▶ DARK ABYSS

 eves.evansauthor

 Eve S Evans Author

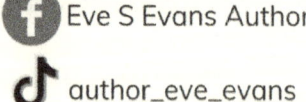 author_eve_evans
TikTok

For exclusive deals, ARCs, and giveaways!

If you love to review books and would like a chance to snatch up one of Eve's ARCs before publication, follow her facebook page or TikTok.

ABOUT
—— THE ——
AUTHOR

From the time I was first published to current, (2021) I've learned so much about life and my journey into the paranormal.

I started this journey a few years ago after living in multiple haunted houses. However, it was one house in particular that chewed me up and spit me out you could say.

After residing in that house I wanted answers... needed them. So I began my journey of interviewing multiple people who too have been haunted. Any occuptaion, you name it, I've interviewed them.

What did I learn from my journey so far? I'm honestly not sure if I will ever get the answers I truly desire in this lifetime. However, I am determined not to stop anytime soon. I will keep plugging along, interviewing and ghost hunting. I am determined to find as many answers as I can in this lifetime before it too is my turn to be nothing but a ghost.

I have several books coming out this year and I am very well known for my "real ghost story anthologies", however, these will be mostly fictional haunted house books as I wanted to give myself a new challenge.

If you'd like to read one of my anthologies my reccomedation to start would be: True Ghost Stories of First Responders. In this book I interview police, firemen, 911 dispatchers and more. They share with me some of their creepiest calls that could possibly even be deemed "ghostly."

Also this year I am hoping to get my paranormal memoir out. I want to share my story and journey with everyone. Until then, just know that if you are terrified in your home or thinking you are going crazy with unexplained occurances, you ARE NOT alone. I thought I was going crazy too. But I wasn't.

If you'd like someone to talk to about what is going on in your home but don't know who to turn to, feel free to message me on Instagram or on Facebook.

Made in the USA
Las Vegas, NV
07 April 2025